His hand was curving around her breast

Should Trent pretend he didn't notice? Casually move his hand? Blame it on the darkness? Or should he wait for Rusty to say something?

"Rusty?"

"Yeees?" She'd noticed.

"Uh, sorry." Trent moved his hand to her shoulder. "It's so dark in here, my aim was a little off. It was an accident."

"Sure it was." Rusty shifted. "The same way I could just reach out like this and *accidentally* grab—"

His heart stopped as she closed her hand around him.

"Well, what do you know? How long have you been like this?" Rusty asked.

"Days," he groaned, then gritted his teeth as her fingers outlined him.

"I'm impressed..."

Dear Reader,

I was flipping through a magazine similar to *Texas Men* when my still-single sister came by to deliver another dispatch from the dating front. "It is so hard to meet eligible men," she complained. And here I sat with a veritable treasure trove of bachelors. I showed her the magazine, bypassing any profiles with the words, *free spirit, no strings* or *open relationship*.

"Take a look at him." I pointed out a nice, salt-of-the-earth sort of man. He looked like the type who was ready to settle down and raise a family. "I wouldn't mind having him for a brother-in-law," I told her.

What followed is pretty much the same conversation Rusty has with her grandmother in chapter one. And—can you believe this—my sister refused, *refused*, to consider answering any of the ads. I have to admit that at this point, I seriously considered answering on her behalf.

I didn't. Instead I wrote *Christmas Male*. I hope you enjoy it, and I guarantee that a copy will be in my sister's Christmas stocking.

Sincerely,

Heather MacAllister

P.S. By the way, if you happen to have an eligible brother or son, or know of anyone who does...

Heather MacAllister
CHRISTMAS MALE

Harlequin Books

TORONTO • NEW YORK • LONDON
AMSTERDAM • PARIS • SYDNEY • HAMBURG
STOCKHOLM • ATHENS • TOKYO • MILAN
MADRID • WARSAW • BUDAPEST • AUCKLAND

To my sister, Allison Wilkes.
I *still* think it would have been a good idea.

ISBN 0-373-25716-3

CHRISTMAS MALE

Copyright © 1996 by Heather W. MacAllister.

1

"Trent, my boy, it's high time you got yourself hitched."

Although he'd been expecting such a comment, Trent Davis Creighton had hoped to escape from this weekend visit to the Triple D Ranch without discussing his future matrimonial prospects with his uncles.

He finished countersigning the papers authorizing him to buy certificates of deposit with the ranch's quarterly oil royalties, then met his uncle Clarence's shrewd brown eyes. "Does this mean you like Miranda?" As Trent spoke, he gazed out the ranch office window where a tall blonde, wearing a wrinkled linen outfit, stood next to his car and waited impatiently for him to drive her back to Dallas.

"Whether or not I like her isn't the point." The leather chair creaked as Clarence shifted his weight, easing his arthritic hip. "The point is that you should be looking for a wife. You're not going to find one in that direction."

Trent had no intention of looking for a wife in any direction, but he'd hoped bringing Miranda with him for the weekend would appease his uncles. "Miranda would make any man a fine wife," Trent found himself saying. And she would—when she was ready for marriage. However, she wasn't, and Trent was honest enough to admit that her disinterest in a permanent commitment was a large part of her attraction for him.

"And so she will," Clarence agreed. "But she's not the type of woman you want for a wife."

"And why not?" Actually, if he was to consider marriage right now—and he most assuredly was not—Trent considered Miranda exactly the sort of wife he'd want. She managed to look classy and sexy at the same time, which appealed to him. He couldn't imagine what his uncles objected to—because he knew if Clarence objected, then Harvey and Doc, Trent's other uncles, objected as well.

"She's a high-maintenance quarter horse. Lots of flash, fast out of the gate, but no stamina."

Trent burst out laughing.

Clarence leveled a look at him. "We've talked to you before about your blondes."

Boot heels striking a wooden floor announced the approach of another one of the uncles. Trent glanced toward the doorway as Doc entered the office.

"What can I say?" Still chuckling, Trent turned to face the most taciturn of his uncles, holding out another set of papers. "I like blondes. Tall blondes." He pointed to the signature line and watched as Doc signed. "And *she*—" he hooked a thumb toward the window"—is a mighty fine blonde."

After scrawling his name, Doc snorted and walked over to the window. "She's got long flanks but a narrow pelvis. Not much breeding room."

Trent was *very* glad Miranda could not hear this conversation.

Doc finished his assessment. "You'll not get more than one or two kids out of her."

Trent grimaced. "You're assuming I want more than one or two children. Besides, you're a vet, not an obstetrician." Why did he let himself get drawn into these discussions?

"A narrow pelvis is a narrow pelvis," Doc stated.

"You have to consider these things, Trent," added Clarence, complacently folding his hands across his ample stomach. "Along with the fact that you'd better get started growing young 'uns before you're too old to enjoy them."

"Point taken." Arguing was fruitless. "Where's Uncle Harvey? I still need his signature on these transfer papers."

"He's looking for a pen," Clarence responded.

"I *have* a pen," Trent said. "Several pens, as I'm sure he knows." He walked to the office door. "Uncle Harvey? It's time Miranda and I left for Dallas. We want to avoid the Sunday afternoon traffic."

From somewhere inside the ranch house, he heard a faint response, but couldn't make it out.

Clarence appeared lost in thought. Doc continued to gaze out the window, probably assessing one of Miranda's other physical traits.

He confirmed this momentarily. "Broad shoulders. I couldn't tell at first because the narrow pelvis skewed the ratio, but with your shoulders, Trent, and hers, your sons—few though there'll likely be—" he glanced at Trent "—should have a good set of shoulders. I'll be able to tell you more after meeting her parents."

No one was going to meet anyone's parents. Trent did not feel any pressing need to get married. He had the Triple D's assets to manage as well as other financial irons in the fire. He was, in fact, on the verge of making his mark in the Dallas financial world and he'd be doing it without Triple D funds, a distinction becoming increasingly important to him.

A wife didn't fit into his plans.

Unfortunately, his uncles didn't agree.

"Uncle Harvey!" Trent called again, wincing as he recognized the impatience in his voice. He loved his uncles and all their endearing quirks. However a man had his limits.

"Might have girls," Clarence said, still pondering Trent's future progeny.

"A possibility," Doc agreed somberly.

Trent was saved from a lecture on the exact mathematical probability by the breathless arrival of Harvey, the remaining Davis brother.

"I found it!" Triumphantly, he held up an angular silver pen. "Trent, this is the same kind of pen used by the NASA astronauts in space. It will write in any direction with or without gravity."

Trent smiled and tapped the third set of papers.

"I thought you ordered one of those last year." Clarence examined the pen.

"Oh, yes, but I gave it to the Miller boy when he graduated. I never got the chance to try it, so I reordered."

"Uncle Harvey, if you would sign your name right here?" Trent prompted.

Harvey retrieved his pen and grabbed for the papers. "It really works. Let me show you." Bending over, he placed the papers against the front of the desk and turned so that he was writing upside down. "There you go, Trent. The ink flows without interruption. Want to try it?"

Trent, already countersigning, shook his head. "Thanks, but I'm using the Executive Compass Pen you got for me the Christmas before last."

Harvey's face lit up. "How has that one performed? As I recall, it was guaranteed for a full year or my money back."

"Fine. It's worked just fine." Or at least it had through the Trent D. Creig part of his name. He pressed harder, but the Ultimate Executive Compass Pen, with tweezers and toothpick, had run out of ink. Irritated, he shook it.

"Been over a year since you bought it?" Clarence asked.

"Yes, but a high-quality product would have lasted longer." Harvey frowned. "A year should have been the minimum."

"It's okay," Trent broke into the discussion, which he knew from experience could last for some time. "I write more than the average person."

"Use the NASA pen." Harvey thrust it at him. "Astronauts depend on them, you know."

"Now that'll be a quality product," Clarence added.

Trent accepted the NASA pen and finished signing his name, quickly packing away the papers before another discussion could boil over. And from the way his uncles were looking at him, he could sense one simmering now.

"I'll, uh, be back in September, if I don't see you all before then." Trent felt unaccountably guilty as three pairs of identical brown eyes, topped by graying bushy eyebrows, gazed at him. Why were they so set on his marrying? He picked up his briefcase and walked from behind the huge wooden desk that had served as the hub of Triple D Ranch business since his grandfather's time.

Clarence leaned forward, and the leather chair creaked. Trent offered a hand to help him stand. Usually Clarence refused, but today he accepted the help.

They're getting older, Trent thought, even as he suspected Clarence was exaggerating his infirmities to lend a sense of urgency to Trent's search for a wife. Still, he thought he smelled horse liniment, which he suspected Doc had prescribed for Clarence's joints. "It's time for me to leave. I've kept Miranda waiting for too long as it is."

"Oh, yes. She appears quite put out," Harvey informed him from the window.

Trent stepped forward, but Clarence held on to his hand. "Keep looking, boy, she isn't the right one."

Trent intended to smile and make some innocuous remark. He *should* have let the comment pass. Instead he blurted, "How do you know she isn't the right one? Other than her narrow pelvis," he added before Doc could.

"She's not a comfortable sort of woman."

"Bony," elaborated Doc.

"That, too," Clarence acknowledged before continuing his lecture. The strength of his grip belied his earlier struggle to stand. "But she wouldn't be happy here at the Triple D."

"We'd live in Dallas," Trent reminded him. He meant his future wife, not necessarily Miranda, but knew it was useless to point that out.

"You won't always live in Dallas. We're getting on in years." Clarence squeezed Trent's arm before releasing it.

"But we're taking good care of ourselves," Harvey broke in. "We take a multivitamin with one hundred percent of the minimum daily requirements for adults over age fifty-five. We exercise on Dr. Pritchard's Healthcycle to raise our heart rates for twenty minutes three times—"

"The boy knows that, Harvey."

Harvey broke off immediately. Clarence rarely interrupted him.

"What we're trying to say is that it's time you looked for a wife. Seriously looked. She should be a willing life partner who isn't afraid of a little work. Someone who'll be a good mother to your children, should you be blessed with them. Feed 'em right, raise 'em straight and keep the home fires burning while you're out supporting your family."

"And she should do it wearing high heels and pearls, right?" As soon as the words were out, Trent regretted them. His uncles meant well, but his marital status was becoming a sore point. "I mean, you've described a housewife from those old television shows."

"And what's wrong with that?"

"It was nearly forty years ago. Modern women aren't like that."

"Not the women you keep company with. You need to find someone like your aunt Emma, may she rest in peace."

Now how was a man supposed to argue with that? Though they'd never had children of their own, Clarence's wife, Emma, had been a mother to Trent since he'd come to live at the Triple D when he was seven years old. Neither Doc nor Harvey had ever married and Emma Davis had taken care of all of them.

"Aunt Emma was one of a kind," Trent said quietly.

"That she was," Clarence said, with murmured agreements from Doc and Harvey. "But that doesn't let you off the hook."

"What do you expect me to do—order a wife from one of your catalogs?"

Doc scratched his chin. "Why not? You can order livestock."

"And I have a catalog." Harvey dashed from the room.

"Why am I not surprised?" Trent muttered to himself.

"I'm glad you brought the subject up." Clarence put on his reading glasses and reached into his pocket just as Harvey galloped back into the room.

"That was quick," Trent said dryly, suspecting he'd been set up.

"Because I'm wearing ultra-gripper track shoes." Harvey raised his foot to reveal a pale gridded sole. "They grip the pavement sixty-seven percent more than the bestselling store brand."

Trent knew better than to point out the lack of pavement at the Triple D Ranch. He was more concerned with the magazine Harvey held. "*Texas Men?* What is this?" Flipping through the glossy publication, he groaned. "It's a giant personals ad. You aren't seriously suggesting that I—"

"'Rancher seeks traditional wife,'" Clarence read from a creased paper.

"What rancher?" Trent asked, suspecting he didn't want to know.

"You, Trent."

"You've got to be kidding."

Clarence peered over his half-glasses.

"I'm not a rancher," Trent insisted.

"It's in your blood, boy." Clearing his throat, Clarence proceeded. "'Although I currently live in Dallas, my heart is in the Texas Hill Country where I'm the only heir to the Triple D Ranch.'"

"Oh, please. You're not—"

Clarence held up his hand and continued reading. "'Living in the city has taught me what's important in life—family, the land and the love of a good woman. Not just any woman, but that one special woman who'll share my life's vision of hearth and home. I'm a simple man who values honesty and hard work. The woman with whom I'd like to share my life should be willing to work right along beside me, raising our children and keeping our home happy and healthy.'"

"You're describing pioneers!" Not only that, Trent hardly considered himself a simple man who loved the land.

Doc pointed. "Read the next bit."

"'I'm aware that this way of life has fallen into disfavor, but I believe that people today are working too hard for too little. Parents are letting others raise their children, resulting in unhappy families. That's why I want to return to the natural order of a male providing and a female nurturing.'"

"What if I don't *want* to be nurtured? What if I don't want to provide so some woman can twiddle her thumbs all day?"

Undeterred, Clarence continued. "'My wife won't have to exhaust herself trying to do my job as well as hers. If you agree and are between the ages of eighteen—'"

"Uncle Clarence, I wouldn't even consider dating an eighteen-year-old!" Trent protested that point, though why, he didn't know. His uncle had just described a politically incorrect nightmare.

Harvey handed Clarence the NASA pen. Clarence made a note. "'Between the ages of twenty-one and thirty... What do you think, Doc? Can we bump that up to thirty-five?"

Doc rubbed the back of his head. "Prime childbearing years are somewhat younger, but with today's medicine..." He shrugged. "Go ahead—and add that it's okay if she has some meat on her bones."

Even given his fond tolerance for his uncles, Trent was speechless. As he listened, Clarence outlined qualities that might describe the daughter of Betty Crocker and Norman Rockwell, concluding with, "'Help me capture the spirit of an old-fashioned country Christmas with all the trimmings here at the Triple D.'"

"Wait a minute—"

"That was my idea," a pleased Harvey inserted.

"'Come prepared to cook up a storm and hang the cholesterol.'"

Doc harumphed.

"That was Clarence's idea," Harvey said.

"'Piano players will be given preference.'"

"For the love of—"

"'The Triple D has a modern, fully equipped kitchen—'"

"With cupochino machine. Don't forget to tell them about my cupochino machine." Harvey pointed to where Clarence should add that information.

"Cappuccino," Trent corrected under his breath.

"Mention the satellite television, too," Harvey instructed.

"That'll be a real draw," Trent muttered.

Clarence made a note. "How does that sound to you, Trent?"

No woman in her right mind will answer that ad. The only responses he was likely to get would be hate mail from feminist groups.

On the other hand, this could be just the answer. The search for a woman who met their outdated criteria would keep his uncles occupied and convince them they were making progress toward getting him married off. When they failed to interest any woman in returning to the Dark Ages, they'd ease up on Trent. In the meantime, he'd be able to concentrate on his business.

A white blur caught his eye. Miranda was stalking back into the house and he didn't blame her. He'd promised her he'd only be a few minutes longer and he didn't want her to overhear them. "I think you've covered just about everything. Look, I've got to leave now." He started for the door. "Take care."

"What about the responses?"

"I'll meet one woman of your choice." Assuming there would be one.

"Now, Trent, son—"

"One." He held up a finger.

Clarence, an old horse trader, knew when to back off. "And you'll promise to come and meet her?"

"Yes."

"For Christmas?" Harvey asked. For all his dithering, Harvey wasn't a bad negotiator, either.

"Yes, for Christmas," Trent promised.

"Two weeks?"

"Uncle Harvey, I can't spare two weeks at the end of the year."

Harvey looked stubborn.

"Not much time to get acquainted with your future wife." Clarence rubbed his hip. Trent refrained from rolling his eyes.

"All right, all right! Two weeks at Christmas." He actually felt guilty since that was one promise he knew he wouldn't have to keep.

RUSTY ROMERO inhaled gratefully as she unlocked the door to her Chicago apartment. Food. She smelled food.

"Gran? Is that you?" Rusty dumped her purse and jacket on the sideboard and kicked off her pumps.

A trim woman with an attractive silver bob stepped to the door of the kitchen. "And who else would be warming a casserole in your kitchen?"

"A *casserole?* How domestic. Did you make it yourself?"

"Certainly." Agnes Romero smiled triumphantly before disappearing inside the kitchen.

"This I've got to see." Rusty followed her grandmother, dropping her portfolio onto the couch on the way.

"Where have you been?" Agnes asked. "It's nine-thirty."

"Working." Rusty slumped against the doorjamb.

Her grandmother shot her a you've-been-working-too-hard look. "I brought the dish over a couple of hours ago, but when you didn't call and *rave* over it, I naturally assumed you could barely stomach it."

"Gran!" Laughing, Rusty shook her head. "What is it this time?"

Wearing cow oven mitts, Agnes removed the rectangular dish. "Tuna noodle casserole."

"For Thanksgiving?" Rusty's grandmother had been testing potential Thanksgiving menus for weeks. It would be the first home-cooked turkey dinner the two had ever shared.

"Of course not. This is a small deviation. Go get comfortable and I'll bring you a plate."

Too tired to protest her grandmother's waiting on her, Rusty collapsed onto her living room sofa.

From in the kitchen came the sound of the silverware drawer being opened. "How's the campaign going?"

"I'm reviewing magazines for the print ads."

"Is this still the shaving lotion?"

"Gran, *please*," Rusty said in mock indignation. "This is much more than mere shaving lotion. This is a complete line of men's grooming essentials based on all-natural ingredients."

"How complete a line can it be?" Agnes Romero stuck her head out the kitchen door. "A man doesn't need anything more than shaving lotion, deodorant and hair dressing."

"They don't call it 'dressing' anymore. It's bio-fixative."

Rusty heard smothered laughter. "Let me guess, there's tinted moisturizer and bronzing gel."

"No bronzing gel. Men have caught on to that. It's 'tan evener.' And there's a cellular eye treatment, as well."

"Tinted?"

"Pine, oak and walnut. Guaranteed to freshen your expression." Rusty flipped open her portfolio and withdrew a stack of publications.

Agnes appeared with a tray. "Put those away and relax for a bit." Setting her burden down on the coffee table in front of the sofa, Rusty's grandmother pushed aside the magazines and sat beside her.

"Thanks, Gran." Rusty reached for the plate. A beige gelatinous lump wiggled in the center.

Agnes frowned. "I've probably seen a hundred recipes, all virtually alike, touting tuna noodle casserole as though it's some nutritional elixir. I thought I'd see what all the fuss is about."

"Have you eaten any yet?" From previous experience Rusty knew that Agnes's culinary efforts were uneven at best.

"Yes." Agnes watched as Rusty propped her feet on the table and scooped a forkful of the casserole. "It lacks a certain visual appeal. Though it was more appealing two hours ago."

"Sorry. If I'd known you were experimenting today, I would have called." She tasted it. "Hmm."

"That's what I thought." Agnes reached for the plate.

"No, no." Rusty held it out of the way. "I'll eat it. It's not bad." Especially since she was starving.

"But it's nothing you feel you lacked in your youth, is it?"

Rusty exhaled. Underneath her grandmother's teasing was a genuine concern. Since Agnes Romero had sold her real estate business and retired a couple of years ago, she'd tried to turn herself into some sort of domestic goddess, apparently feeling the need to atone for not being one during Rusty's childhood. "No. I don't feel I was deprived of *anything* in my youth." She gripped her grandmother's hand for emphasis.

"Well, that's a relief. I'll never have to make this dish again."

They both laughed.

"What happened to all the Thanksgiving experiments?" Rusty fondly remembered the two glorious weeks her grandmother learned to make pies.

"Oh, I'm still working on the ultimate menu, but I found references to tuna fish in the 'family favorites' section of *Holiday Hearth and Home* and I just..." She trailed off with a shrug.

"And you just felt guilty because you didn't give me an apple-pie childhood in the suburbs." Rusty set the plate down and hugged her grandmother. "I had a *great* childhood. You taught me survival skills for the big city. How many seven-year-olds can order a complete, nutritionally balanced meal for two? *And* calculate the tip?"

Agnes chuckled. "How many seven-year-olds have to?" She leaned back. "I suppose that since I retired, I've had time to think about my life. And I'll admit that I have a few regrets. When I see you and the kind of life you lead now, I see myself."

Rusty knew what was bothering her grandmother. "And you don't want me to have regrets, too, is that it?"

Agnes nodded.

"Hey, no problem. I love my life. It's *perfect* for me right now. I'm at my ideal weight and have no wrinkles. How many people can say that?"

"But you work so hard."

"So did you! At least I'm not out showing houses on weekends." Rusty retrieved the plate and continued eating the casserole. "Now look, this isn't bad, but do you really think it's a substitute for having my own dessert named after me at a four-star restaurant?"

Agnes groaned. "I should have been home more for you. I've made the same mistakes with you that I did with your mother."

"Oh, I disagree. You made completely different mistakes with me."

At her grandmother's startled expression, Rusty burst out laughing. "I don't think you made mistakes with either one of us," she said firmly. "You made choices."

Agnes looked pensive. "But sometimes I wonder if I should have made other choices."

"Nonsense." Rusty had finished inhaling the casserole. "I'm going to make some coffee. Want some?"

"This late you'd better make decaf."

Rusty walked into the kitchen. She'd planned to put in a few more hours of work before bed and definitely needed the caffeine. She'd have to make a new pot after her grandmother left. "Decaf it is," she called.

Pulling open the refrigerator door to get out the coffee beans, she discovered a foreign plastic container. "What's this in the fridge?"

"I tried to make a pecan pie and it didn't set," her grandmother called out. "But the filling tastes great over ice cream."

It looked like it would, too. "I don't have any ice cream."

"Yes, you do."

Rusty yanked open the freezer to find a carton of the most expensive brand of vanilla ice cream. She sighed in bliss. "Now, how can a woman of such perception and insight feel regrets about anything?"

"You always could be swayed with food," her grandmother replied.

"All too true."

When Rusty returned with the coffee and two bowls of pecan-topped ice cream, she found her grandmother flipping through the pages of one of the men's magazines Rusty had brought home.

"These are quite enlightening," her grandmother said.

"Any one in particular?" Rusty asked, taking a heavenly mouthful of ice cream.

"*This* one." Agnes held up a copy of *Texas Men*.

"Ah, the beefcake mag. Can you believe it? Men actually advertising for dates?" Rusty snickered.

"Oh, I don't know..." Trailing off, her grandmother studied some of the profiles. "Rusty, darling, have you ever considered writing to one of these men?"

"Oh, Gran, please!"

"Don't be hasty...I see a six-foot-four, brown-eyed brunet—"

"What's the matter with him?"

"*Nothing.* It says that he's built a construction business and hasn't had time to meet women."

"Yeah, right."

"Seriously, doesn't he attract you at all?" Agnes held out the picture.

"Nope."

"All your hard work is suppressing your hormones. This one's five-eight, but he's really cute."

"Gran, ask yourself what kind of man has to advertise to meet women?"

"It appears that busy, vibrant and successful men do. Look." She pointed to a photograph of an admittedly attractive man.

His picture was a typical businessman's studio pose and yet something about his eyes caught Rusty's attention. "I look like this because it's expected, but this isn't the real me," they said. And, she had to admit, there was a definite invitation to "meet the real me" there. In fact, she wondered where the "real me" lived.

"See?" Her grandmother smiled slyly.

"Okay, he's cute." Quite attractive. Definitely worth a second look. "What's the matter with him?"

"Rusty!"

Rusty set down her bowl and grabbed for the magazine. After a brief struggle, Agnes let go.

"Aha! 'Rancher seeks *traditional* wife.' He doesn't look like a rancher to me." Not that she knew any ranchers. However, Rusty's eyes widened as she read the biographical profile. "Did you see this? He's a Neanderthal! The missing link!"

"Rusty, darling—"

Rusty waved her grandmother into silence. "Listen to this—'That's why I want to return to the natural order of a *male providing and a female nurturing.*' No wonder this guy isn't married. Can you say 'domestic slavery'?" Rusty tossed the magazine back to her grandmother and cleared away their dishes.

"All right, I'll admit his ideas are unilluminated—"

"Ha! He's setting women's rights back a hundred years! Two hundred, even."

"But read the part about going to his ranch and having an old-fashioned Christmas."

"'Old-fashioned' meaning women do all the work."

With half an ear, Rusty listened as her grandmother read about cutting a Christmas tree, sleigh rides and caroling. "Oh, and he wants someone who can play the piano."

"When would she have time?" Rusty grumbled on her way back to the living room.

"And—" Agnes glanced toward Rusty "—a woman with meat on her bones."

What patronizing nerve! Rusty's mouth opened and closed. Finally she shook her head. "I *pity* the poor woman who hooks up with that guy!" Incensed, she paced in front of her grandmother. "In fact, Mr. King of the Neanderthals should be reported to somebody in human rights. There's got to be a committee somewhere. Can you believe him?" She stared down at the man's picture. He couldn't be an *unattractive* jerk, oh, no. A shame those eyes had to be wasted on him. "Any woman responding to that profile needs therapy."

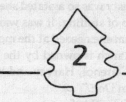

"You RESPONDED to the chauvinistic rancher?" Rusty stared at her grandmother over a golden brown but overcooked Thanksgiving turkey. "How funny. Why didn't you tell me? I would've loved to have been in on the joke."

"It wasn't a joke." Her grandmother's serious blue eyes met hers.

Rusty waited, but Agnes didn't crack a smile. "Come on, Gran, you're scaring me."

"And I wasn't the only respondent. There are plenty of women ready to forsake the rat race. But I, or rather, we—*you*, actually—are the one the Davis brothers have invited for Christmas. Naturally, I'd come with you to chaperone."

Spend Christmas on a ranch with strangers who wanted to check her out as housewife material? Her grandmother *had* to be joking. "You turned them down, right?"

Agnes shook her head. "I don't want to turn them down."

Rusty's silverware clattered in the silence. "Let me get this straight. You answered a personals ad *in my name* and now you want me to meet this man?"

Agnes stared at her plate. "Yes, but I knew that I'd need to talk to you first."

"Darn right!" Rusty was so agitated she helped herself to another glob of stuffing. It was warm, soft and full of fat—just what she needed at the moment.

"The Triple D Ranch is owned by the three Davis brothers. There's Clarence, Harvey and William, but everybody calls him Doc."

"I don't want to hear this."

"Trent is their nephew."

"Send them my condolences."

"Rusty."

Rusty abandoned the stuffing. "I'm sorry, Gran. This isn't like you and I don't understand."

Agnes began clearing away the remains of an opulent Thanksgiving feast. She'd prepared far too much food for just the two of them, and Rusty had been happily looking forward to leftovers. "Their description of Christmas on the ranch sounded like my girlhood on the farm."

"You couldn't wait to leave the farm," Rusty reminded her. She looked around her grandmother's elegantly contemporary apartment. "I can't even imagine you on a farm."

"Oh, but there were good things about the country. And we'd have the same things on the ranch—a *real* Christmas tree that we'd cut ourselves. Popcorn and cranberry strings, carols, hot chocolate . . . and family." Smiling, her grandmother looked off into the distance.

"Hold it. We are not related to those people."

To Rusty's shock, her grandmother's eyes grew moist. "I want to go, Rusty. I *want* an old-fashioned

Christmas. I want *you* to have an old-fashioned Christmas at least once."

This suddenly sentimental woman was not the grandmother who had raised her. Rusty managed a shaky laugh. "I'm going to take away all your home and craft magazines. They're an evil influence."

Agnes ignored her. "Couldn't you spare a couple of weeks?"

Said that way, it sounded like such a small request. But it wasn't. "You're not asking for just any two weeks. That's when Dearsing is reviewing the Next to Nature campaigns." Rusty gestured helplessly. "I've got to be there and make sure mine is the most dynamic presentation that Dearsing has ever seen. This campaign could go national and I want it so bad, Gran. I just can't take those two weeks off."

The light went out of Agnes's eyes. "Of course you can't. I was foolish to suggest it."

Rusty felt awful. Worse than awful. She owed her grandmother for the years Agnes had spent raising her. Now her grandmother had retired, and Rusty had vowed to see that she would be financially secure for the rest of her life. Landing the Next to Nature campaign would mean a promotion and a salary increase. She couldn't jeopardize this opportunity. "Not foolish—just unrealistic. I mean, I can't cook."

"He doesn't have to know that."

"It'd be obvious fairly quickly."

Agnes gestured to the table. "*I've* learned to cook. I could teach you—or do all the cooking for you."

She was completely sincere. Rusty could see it in her eyes. "That's deceitful."

"A grandmother helping her granddaughter in the kitchen? I don't think so."

"Even if you did, I'm not anything like the woman he describes, thank heavens."

"How do you know you aren't if you've never given it a try?" Agnes headed for the kitchen.

"Because I have my own career and don't feel like giving it all up to wait hand and foot on some man." Shuddering, Rusty picked up the turkey and followed her. "Gran, we don't need to go play house at this ranch. The two of us will have a great Christmas together, just like always."

"Of course we will." Her smile tight-lipped, Agnes began scraping the plates.

Rusty couldn't stand it. For some unfathomable reason, her grandmother had her heart set on spending Christmas at the Triple D Ranch and she couldn't go unless Rusty agreed to go, too.

How unappealing.

On the other hand, it would be an opportunity to strike a blow for womankind by enlightening a certain Texas rancher to the realities of modern life. And, too, her grandmother was bound to lose interest in cooking three meals a day for all those men. Rusty predicted a four-day stay, tops. By then, her grandmother would have gotten over this domestic nonsense.

Four days. Hmm. Rusty could steal four days, if she took her laptop computer with fax modem and her printer with her. It would be worth the time away to have her grandmother back to normal, though Rusty'd miss sampling the cooking experiments.

"Oh, all right, Gran," she said as if granting a great concession. "If you want to go, we'll give it a shot. But we're only going because *you* want to. Don't get any ideas about me hooking up with this relic from the Dark Ages."

STUNNED, Trent hung up the telephone after talking to his gleefully euphoric uncles. There were some pretty desperate women out there, judging by the letters they said they'd received. And now he had to meet one of them. *And* her grandmother. At the worst possible time.

Leaning his chair back on two legs, Trent gazed out from the window in his twenty-second-floor corner office onto the Dallas skyline.

His uncles expected him for two weeks at Christmas. Two weeks. And he'd promised. It didn't matter that he'd never expected to have to keep it, he'd given his word.

Just to his left was an easel with an artist's rendering of the proposed Ridge Haven Retirement Village— Trent's personal project. He'd invested everything into it—both time and money. The entire package of bids and financing had to be in place by December thirty-first. To be away for two weeks at this crucial time was impossible.

And breaking a promise to his uncles was unthinkable.

Perhaps he could still manage to satisfy everybody by meeting this woman and failing to be impressed by either her or her domestic talents. That's the tack he'd take. Polite indifference. He would not seek her out or otherwise encourage her. A few days of hard work on an isolated ranch with no husband in sight would send Miss Suzy Homemaker running back to—he checked his notes—Chicago before they could say "Jingle Bells." By the end of the week he'd be back in Dallas.

Now all he'd have to do was find a way to stay in touch with his office . . . people telecommuted all the time. There was no reason he couldn't do it, too. He'd have to.

"THEY'RE COMING! I can see them through my aluminum, ten-magnification binoculars!"

Harvey's excitement was mirrored by Trent's other uncles. He'd never seen them like this. Even Doc smiled, and Trent, though still skeptical of this entire scheme, was glad he'd come.

"Harvey, those binoculars beat the Junior Astronomer telescope." Clarence patted the tripod next to him. "Better make a note."

Harvey's face fell. "Can't I meet the Romero ladies first?"

"Only proper," Doc growled.

"Of course, of course. We'll all greet the ladies. Won't we, Trent?"

"Sure, Uncle Clarence."

Teeth gritted, Trent smiled and followed them as they went to stand on the front porch. He'd decided to play his polite though indifferent role to the hilt. No matter how enthusiastic his uncles were, these poor women had been lured here under false pretenses and the sooner they left, the sooner Trent could get back to work. He'd return for Christmas Day—maybe even manage Christmas Eve, too, if all went well.

Trent watched a small, nondescript blue car trail a cloud of dust into the ranch yard. Conscious that he was about to meet a species of female with whom he had no adult experience—the kind who aspired to drive a minivan full of children—he pondered his approach to her. He couldn't make himself be deliberately rude. That wasn't his way and it wasn't this poor woman's fault that he'd been misrepresented. This situation was entirely his own doing and he was annoyed with himself for allowing it to happen.

The car stopped. "Go open their doors for them, Trent."

Trent almost laughed. For all their talk about it being time for him to marry, his uncles still dispensed instructions as though he were a boy.

Trent deliberately approached the passenger side, guessing that the grandmother would not be the driver.

Opening the door, he reached down expecting to grasp a gnarled hand and help a gray-haired lady wearing an apron and support hose to stand.

Slim legs encased in designer jeans swung toward him and one ankle-booted foot collided with his shin. "Sorry."

Not only didn't the voice quiver with age, it didn't sound sorry at all. Trent refrained from rubbing his leg and gazed down at the car's occupant instead.

A chestnut-haired woman, head cocked to one side, stared back. Raising an eyebrow, she asked, "Going to let me out of the car, or don't I pass inspection?"

Trent backed away. Obviously this wasn't the woman who'd responded to the *Texas Men* profile. The thought actually crossed his mind that some feminist group had come to stage a protest.

The woman stood. Trent noted immediately that she was a fair height. Since he was six-three himself, he liked tall women and never understood men of his height who liked tiny ones. A guy could strain his neck looking down all the time. Even kissing was more effort than it was worth. As for sleeping with them, forget it.

She wore a vest over a blouse with big sleeves, but as far as Trent could tell, she was possessed of at least an adequate figure.

She slammed the car door with enough force to let him know she was put out with him. There might be some justification there, he acknowledged. He wasn't normally so obvious about checking out a woman, but this wasn't a normal situation.

Before he could atone for his rudeness, she stuck out her hand. "Hi, I'm Rusty Romero."

Romero. These were the women who'd been corresponding with his uncles, all right. "Trent Creighton," he replied as he attempted to adjust his mental picture with a surprisingly pleasant reality.

Her hand shook his firmly. It was the handshake of a woman used to shaking hands. He tested his theory by turning his wrist slightly so he would have the superior position.

Rusty resisted and maintained the handshake as one between equals. Her eyes never left his.

Her reaction disoriented him. He'd met women like her. Women who'd had to fight for respect in the construction contracting industry, a field dominated by men. Trent dealt with these women very well, because he didn't consider them women. They were business adversaries or allies. Gender neutral.

But this woman was here in a domestic capacity. Home and hearth. Raising children. Nurturing. Very gender specific.

Housewives had certainly changed since those fifties television shows.

"Shall we call it a draw, or adjourn to the hood of the car where we can arm wrestle?" she asked.

Trent released her hand immediately. "The offer's tempting, but I'll pass."

"You're sure?" That eyebrow of hers was still raised. It had a high arch that lent itself to raising. "I wouldn't want to violate any local greeting customs."

"Around here, we generally don't arm wrestle until the second meeting."

"And what do you wrestle on the third meeting?"

This was no meek Betty Crocker wannabe. Had his uncles been conned? Trent glanced over to see how they were faring and received a second shock.

A well-dressed woman, looking just like any corporate executive's wife Trent had ever seen, chatted with the three men.

He glanced back to Rusty and found her watching him, her lips curved in a superior smile. "My grandmother, Agnes."

"Really?" He looked at the woman again. "She doesn't look the way I pictured." He meant it as a compliment. Rusty didn't take it that way.

"Probably because she left her apron and rolling pin in the car."

"With yours?" he replied, goaded.

"I assumed you'd have one I could borrow," she said after a pause.

"Of course," Trent assured her, though he honestly had no idea whether the Triple D kitchen boasted a rolling pin or not.

It was apparent that Rusty Romero had disliked him on sight. This should have cheered him, but inexplicably, it didn't. He hadn't been at his best during this critical first meeting, however Trent had not reached the age of thirty-three without being unaware of how to charm a woman, even one as prickly as Rusty.

Putting a little extra into his smile, he managed a belated, "Welcome to the Triple D." *That was lame.* Surely he could have done better.

Apparently Rusty thought so, too. "Thanks." She reached back inside the car and retrieved her purse and the keys.

Trent was annoyed with both himself and her. She was supposed to be some meek and mousy homebody who would be dazzled by him and by her good fortune in being selected to visit the Triple D. He'd expected a tenacious husband-hunter and had planned to very carefully, yet firmly, discourage her.

It appeared that this Rusty Romero would need no discouraging at all. That fact chafed at him a bit.

"Shall we unload the luggage?" Trent held out his hand for the keys to the trunk.

After a brief hesitation, Rusty surrendered them. "I'd better warn you that we didn't travel light this trip."

"I've never known a woman to travel light," Trent said without thinking. He popped open the trunk lid to reveal a crammed interior.

"I travel light when it's called for," Rusty snapped. "However, complying with your requirements for an old-fashioned Christmas and a two-week stay resulted in extra baggage."

This was not going to work. Trent had known that, but presumably this woman had been hoping to find a soul mate and life partner. Her attitude was incomprehensible.

Trent propped his hand on the open trunk lid and leveled his gaze at her. "If you didn't want to 'comply with my requirements,' then why are you here?"

"I—" She broke off abruptly, her eyes darting toward her grandmother. When she spoke again, her tone was entirely different. Softer. Conciliatory.

Suspicious.

"I've found that men are eager to appreciate a woman's efforts, yet have no idea of the tools, if you will, required to do the job."

Her big brown eyes challenged him to understand. "We received...conflicting instructions from your uncles."

Oh, no. Trent could only imagine, not that he wanted to. No wonder she'd arrived annoyed.

"My uncles get a bit enthusiastic at times." He looked at them and couldn't help smiling. Harvey was showing his NASA pen to the grandmother. She studied it carefully, pleasing both Harvey and Trent.

"So does my grandmother," Rusty said unexpectedly.

Trent grinned down at her just as she smiled up at him. It was a perfect moment of mutual understanding.

It was also the moment Trent realized that Rusty Romero had a dangerous smile. Her full lips stretched widely, revealing her top teeth in a flawless white crescent. The smile spoke of uninhibited pleasure and her lips...

Trent had never considered himself a lip man before. No, he was more an everything else man. But there was something about Rusty Romero's lips that invited further study—preferably at much closer quarters.

As her smile faded, Trent was reminded of the circumstances. "I'm sorry for the crack about your luggage," he said.

"It's okay. You were just buying into a stereotype."

She made him sound as though he were incapable of thinking for himself. The perfect moment of understanding evaporated. Trent lifted out the top suitcase.

"I'll get this one." Rusty reached for a flat case.

It looked for all the world like— "Is that a laptop?"

Clutching it to her, Rusty regarded him warily. "Yes."

"What do you need that for?"

"Recipes," she answered quickly.

"What happened to three-by-five cards in a plastic box?"

Rusty blinked and her eyebrows drew together. "You mean, diskettes?"

"No, I . . ." Shaking his head, Trent reached for another suitcase. "I didn't realize domestic science had entered the computer age."

"I imagine there are a lot of things you don't realize," Rusty responded, and turned toward the house.

THAT WENT WELL, Rusty thought. She'd established that she was no meek domestic slave to be ordered around and had even embarked on a little enlightening.

By apologizing, Trent had proved he was trainable. He might even be salvageable, and Rusty wouldn't mind claiming salvage rights.

She hadn't realized he was so tall. Of course she'd read his profile and description in *Texas Men*, memorized them in fact, but had expected some exaggeration. No, this man was every bit six-three and didn't need to exaggerate anything. Reality was enough to make a woman catch her breath—but not enough to sign up for the lifestyle he wanted.

No, Rusty shouldn't forget her primary mission here was to enlighten—both her grandmother and these men. She had no doubt the uncles shared their nephew's views of women.

She glanced at them as she headed toward the ranch house, then changed course. Might as well meet them now.

"Here's my granddaughter." Agnes beamed at her.

Maintaining a pleasant expression, Rusty shifted her laptop to her left hand and held out her right to the nearest uncle, prepared to engage in the same maneuvering she'd done with Trent.

"This is Clarence." Her grandmother indicated a portly gentleman with a fair quantity of nearly white hair.

Rusty smiled up into a pair of eyes that looked exactly like Trent's, or the way Trent's would look in thirty or forty years. They were friendly, but shrewd. Glancing quickly at the other men, Rusty surmised that Clarence was in charge.

"Welcome to the Triple D." Clarence spoke with a lot more sincerity than his nephew had. His grip was warm, strong and cordial.

"Thank you." Rusty responded with an abundance of pleasantry and wondered if behavior modification techniques would have any effect on Trent.

"I'll run your bags into the house." Trent's look told her he'd heard her gushing thanks and didn't care one way or the other.

Clarence took over the introductions. "This is Doc." He indicated the man on the other side of Agnes. Because the ratio of gray to white in his hair was in favor of gray, Rusty guessed that this uncle was younger. When she met his eyes, she was prepared for the family resemblance, but Doc barely shook her hand or met her gaze before stepping back.

"And this is my brother, Harvey."

The third Davis brother skipped shaking Rusty's hand altogether. "Is that a laptop?" He pointed to the computer, his eyes bright and childlike.

"Uh." Rusty looked down as though surprised to find herself holding it. "Yes."

"How fast is it?" he asked.

"It's a one hundred thirty-three megahertz Pentium." Let him put that in his pipe and smoke it.

He nodded. "How many megs of RAM?"

"Sixteen, expandable to sixty-four." Rusty had no idea if any of this meant anything to Harvey or not. Her laptop was her pride and joy.

"And the hard disk?"

"Uh, it's a one point three gig." A quick glance around revealed that everybody was smiling, so Rusty described her computer and discussed the assorted peripherals with Harvey.

To her amazement, he was quite knowledgeable. "I have some computer catalogs. Would you mind if we looked up this model?"

"I—sure." What an odd request. "Are you in the market for a computer?"

"I'm always in the market." Harvey dashed off, nearly colliding with Trent, who was carrying another load of their luggage.

"Oh, dear. We should help him," Agnes fluttered, though Rusty had never heard her flutter before.

"Nonsense," Clarence said. "Exercise will do the boy good. Sits behind a desk too much as it is."

"I thought he lived here," Rusty said.

"We'd like for him to live here, but he insists on staying in Dallas."

"Because he works in Dallas," Trent muttered as he walked past. Rusty heard him, but she wasn't certain the others had. "And this is the last of the luggage."

The group turned and followed him to the ranch house.

And that had been another surprise. Rusty had expected some modest homestead, but instead she found herself facing a two-story, columned, brick and white-painted wood house that could have been in any well-to-do Chicago neighborhood. Within sight, but not too close, was a barn and two more buildings she didn't know the purpose of. A few cows grazed in a nearby pasture, but there wasn't a sign of the thundering herds of longhorns Rusty had been expecting.

Dusty plains with cactus and tumbleweeds were missing, too. Instead, the house was surrounded by gently rolling hills and a thicket of trees. The weather was mild enough that Rusty hadn't bothered to put on her jacket. It was a refreshing change from this time of year in Chicago.

She threw back her head and breathed deeply. She'd been working hard and actually could use a break. A long weekend here wouldn't be so bad.

Rusty climbed the steps and crossed the porch, entering the front door in time to hear Harvey's voice.

"And they adjust vertically, as well."

Harvey was demonstrating a forest green leather recliner, one of three. The others were in black and burgundy. "Let me show you." As Rusty watched, her grandmother sat in the chair. Harvey flipped open a panel in the arm and began pressing buttons.

The back dipped and the front extended, supporting Agnes's feet.

"Feel that lumbar support," he said as he pressed another button.

"Oh-hh." Her grandmother sighed and closed her eyes. "Wonderful."

"Do you want to try, Miss Rusty?"

Miss Rusty. Charmed, Rusty sat in the burgundy recliner. Within seconds, Harvey had manipulated the chair into an admittedly comfortable position.

Rusty relaxed her neck—and found that she was staring directly at a big-screen TV turned to a home shopping channel. At the moment, a woman with red fingernails modeled cubic zirconia dinner rings at only $99 and going fast.

"Uncle Harvey, perhaps Rusty and her grandmother would like to see their rooms," Trent prompted, stepping into her line of sight.

As he spoke, Rusty watched his gaze sweep the length of her body. He probably wasn't even aware he was doing it. However, Rusty had to admit that being in a reclining position in front of an admittedly handsome rancher who had just given her the once-over was awakening her hibernating libido.

She sat up and fluffed the back of her hair. Trent's eyes followed the movement of her arms.

Interesting. She swung her legs down and stood.

"Here, I'll lower the footrest for you." Trent reached for the control panel on the chair.

Rusty deliberately leaned toward him so that he'd brush against her. She was testing the chemistry, just for the record.

For the record, the chemistry was combustible. His chest brushed her cheek and shoulder and sent tingles of awareness throughout her upper body.

"Sorry, didn't mean to crowd you there." He smiled down at her and moved away.

Rusty wanted to move with him.

Wasn't this a pleasant surprise? Or maybe not. She remembered staring at his picture and the way his ad had managed to provoke such heightened emotions in her. True, those emotions had been primarily outrage, but she'd always known indifference was the relationship-killing emotion.

She wasn't indifferent to Trent and suspected that he wasn't indifferent to her, either.

"Shall I show you your room now?"

"That would be great. Are we sharing?"

Trent cleared his throat. "No. I put your grandmother in the guest room. Harvey will be testing orthopedic mattresses in the storage barn, so you'll get his room."

"I wouldn't feel right about making your uncle sleep in the barn," Rusty said pointedly. If anybody should be sleeping in the barn, it should be Trent.

Trent chuckled. "It's not what you're thinking. When this ranch was bigger, extra hands used to bunk out there. Unless the weather turns nasty, he'll be fine."

"Are you sure?"

"Let's put it this way. He'd be testing those mattresses whether you were here or not."

"Okay. And where will you be?" she asked casually.

Trent's gaze flicked over her face and lingered on her mouth. "Down the hall from you." He gestured toward the door on the other side of the den, allowing her grandmother to precede them. The uncles remained.

He's being nice now, but don't forget what he really thinks about women, Rusty reminded herself as "not indifferent" slipped into "definitely interested." *Your mission is to enlighten.*

But couldn't she enlighten by demonstrating how a modern woman took charge of her own sexuality? A little short-term dalliance might be beneficial for all concerned. As long as she was away for these few days, shouldn't she make the most of this break? She'd return to Chicago rested and refreshed and with certain tensions eased.

As she walked past him, Rusty wondered if Trent was tense. Conscious of his presence directly behind her, Rusty put a little extra sway in her hips as she followed her grandmother across the room.

Just before she walked through the doorway, she heard Doc's voice.

"Nice, wide pelvis."

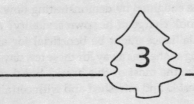

3

"THIS KNIFE is so sharp you can cut a tomato thin enough to read a newspaper through it." Harvey turned to pick up another gadget in a never-ending display of kitchen gadgetry that should be a shoo-in for the infomercial hall of fame.

"When are they going to leave us alone?" Rusty muttered to Agnes. She couldn't believe that just an hour after their arrival, she and her grandmother were apparently expected to produce the evening meal.

Agnes saw nothing wrong with this thinking and had come prepared with homemade goodies she'd perfected in the weeks after Thanksgiving.

Harvey was giving them the grand tour of the kitchen, eye-boggling in its selection of modern appliances, though he was getting a bit too detailed for Rusty.

"And this is the Radish Rosetter," he continued, showing them a metal contraption that looked like a Medieval instrument of torture.

If they wanted their radishes rosetted, they could do it themselves, Rusty grumbled silently.

Clarence and Doc watched from the sidelines, chiming in only for major appliances. Trent, his arms crossed, kept a watchful eye from the butcher block island.

During a demonstration of the vegetable curler, which cut potatoes, carrots and the like into spirals for no practical reason Rusty could discern, she stole a look at him.

A small line appeared between his eyebrows and he seemed ready to intervene at any moment.

When his eyes caught hers, they held that same look of wary concern. He was probably afraid she'd insult his eccentric but endearing uncle.

Detaching herself from the gadgetfest that held her grandmother entranced, Rusty wandered over to stand by Trent. "Don't look so worried," she said in an undertone. "I won't hurt his feelings."

"Or run screaming into the night?"

Rusty almost laughed out loud. "Hey, anybody who knows as much about computers as he does can be allowed certain idiosyncrasies."

The rigid set of Trent's shoulders softened and he uncrossed his arms. "I don't think he actually understands how to operate one. But if something is made for sale, Harvey knows about it."

"And has already purchased it, no doubt."

"Being a consumer is his hobby." Trent grinned, revealing shallow dimples on either side of his mouth. Rusty had never considered dimples particularly masculine—until now. They disappeared quickly as Trent's face relaxed into a pleasant expression.

"So, when do you expect your dinner to be ready?" Rusty changed the subject, mainly to remind herself why she was currently standing in a strange kitchen hundreds of miles from home.

"How long will it take you to cook it?"

Tripped up already. "I have no idea," she said truthfully.

"What are you cooking?"

Rusty wished she'd paid more attention to the goodies her grandmother had packed. As she watched, the little group abandoned the gadget drawer. Doc was demonstrating the cappuccino machine. At least Rusty was assured of decent coffee while she was here. But she still didn't know what was on tonight's menu. "Dinner," she said, "will be a surprise."

"Have you looked in the refrigerator yet? I think Harvey stocked it." Trent pushed away from the butcher block and yanked open the door of the biggest refrigerator Rusty had seen outside of a restaurant kitchen.

A large foil-wrapped lump gleamed at her with golden familiarity. "A spiral-sliced ham! Is that for Christmas dinner?"

"I haven't a clue." Trent poked through the shelves. "There's a turkey in here, as well. Take your pick."

Rusty murmured a heartfelt thank-you to the kitchen gods. "I vote for the ham." Very difficult to ruin something already cooked.

Trent obligingly hauled it out. "It must weigh thirty-five pounds."

"At least. It's as big as the one we get for the office Christmas party." Rusty was uncrinkling the wrapper so she could read the heating instructions and had spoken without thinking.

"Office? You work?"

She hesitated. Well, why not admit it? "Yes."

"As what? A secretary?"

It was the way he said it, as though he couldn't imagine a woman being anything else. Not that being a secretary was anything to be ashamed of—Rusty had worked as a secretary during the summers between college terms. It was just that a secretary was one of the three occupations—teaching and nursing being the other two—that had, until recently, been considered the only suitable work for women.

She knew her grandmother had struggled for acceptance in the real estate business, scraping out a living with commissions on the smaller properties while the larger listings—and commissions—went to men who needed the income to support their families. But Agnes had been supporting a family, too.

Trent's comment brought it all back to Rusty. She, herself, had not had to struggle because women like her grandmother had blazed the trail for her. Obviously her grandmother's work wasn't finished, though for some reason she was in regression at the moment.

It was up to Rusty to carry on.

Trent had turned away and was looking into a cabinet, obviously not even interested in Rusty's response. *The only work that's important is man's work.* He might as well have shouted the words aloud.

"This ought to hold it." He pulled out a roasting pan and smiled at her, the creases dimpling attractively.

Rusty's breath caught before she hardened her heart.

Dimples or not, Trent had a lot to learn.

"KISS THE COOK?" Rusty looked down at the apron she wore. "I hope they don't take this as a suggestion."

"We don't have time for subtlety, dear." Agnes, with her cow oven mitts and matching apron that said Udder Delight, breezed past carrying a green bean casserole.

"*Subtlety?* What are you talking about?"

"Trent Creighton, Rusty. I can't believe some smart cookie hasn't snapped up such a handsome young man."

"I can," Rusty muttered. She'd agreed to come here so her grandmother could get all this domestic nostalgia out of her system. Granted, ostensibly, the purpose of their visit was so Rusty and Trent could get to know each other. But her grandmother couldn't *seriously* believe Rusty would consider leading the kind of life Trent wanted to live. She'd *told* her so. Repeatedly.

But obviously, ineffectively.

"Rachel Marie Romero, you have the opportunity of a lifetime here and I intend to see that you make the most of it!" Agnes punctuated her words by slapping her oven mitts on the counter. "You have to be prepared to use all the feminine ammunition you've got."

Rusty intended to use feminine ammo, all right. But she and her grandmother had different targets in mind. Her grandmother would assume she was aiming for Trent's heart. Instead, Rusty was trying to shoot holes in his overinflated ego.

Eyeing her grandmother's outfit—the ruffled pinafore top was really too much—Rusty decided the Kiss-the-Cook apron wasn't so bad after all. "Hey, look." She pointed to the casserole. "I cooked something!"

A buzzer sounded and Agnes whizzed past. "Canned green beans, canned cream of mushroom soup and canned fried onions mixed together *barely* counts."

Rusty made a sound of protest. "Didn't I open those cans all by myself?"

Her grandmother pulled open the oven door and withdrew cornbread muffins that she'd baked back in Chicago and had just warmed in the oven with the ham. "Oh, I hope this will do for our first dinner," she fretted. "We should have cooked something really impressive instead of using the ham." Shooting Rusty an accusing look, she shut the oven door.

"They should have given us more notice. And the ham was just sitting there." Rusty returned to cutting tomatoes for the salad. "If they hadn't wanted us to serve it, then why was it in the refrigerator?"

"Maybe they were saving it for Christmas dinner. Or maybe it was a gift for somebody else."

"Trent *said* we could use it."

The mention of Trent's name mollified Agnes somewhat.

"There's a turkey in there, too. We won't have to go to the grocery store for a while." Rusty laid a slice of tomato on the green bean can label and tried to read through it. By golly, Harvey was right. She could see dark lines, but the words were blurry. The tomato slice was limp, though, and disintegrated before she could get it into the salad bowl. She was concentrating so completely, her grandmother's silence didn't register immediately. When it did, she glanced back over her shoulder and caught her grandmother's stare.

Agnes immediately looked away.

"What?" Rusty asked, suspicious.

"Nothing." Her grandmother spread a cloth in the bread basket.

"There's something." Rusty carried the salad bowl over to the butcher block island. "Something about grocery shopping?"

Agnes turned around and peered into the oven.

"You can't see through foil. What gives?"

"Well, Rusty." Agnes straightened and wiped her hands on the terry cow-trimmed hand towel attached to her pocket. "This *is* a rural area."

"So we'll have to drive a few miles and do all our shopping at once. We can do that. It's a matter of step-by-step planning." Rusty excelled at planning.

"This is a ranch. They grow their own food."

"They didn't grow that spiral-sliced ham."

"No, but I did see chickens."

"Did you? Were they in the freezer?"

"Not yet."

"What do you—oh! That's awful! No way." Holding out her hands, Rusty backed up. "There is no way I'm touching one of those chickens. A live chicken—clucking. I couldn't—and the feathers, what happens to those?" She waved her hands. "No. Don't tell me. I can't think about it."

"Rusty..." Agnes advanced toward her.

"No! Absolutely not!"

"Absolutely not what?" Rusty heard just before backing into someone. Trent, of course.

Strong arms clasped around her, a sensation she might have enjoyed if she hadn't been so revolted by the thought of murdering chickens.

"Steady there."

Rusty whirled around and launched into an immediate attack. "If there's to be any chicken necks wrung, they'll have to be wrung by somebody else. I prefer mine wrapped in plastic."

"You smother your chickens then?" Trent grinned.

"Ye-ees," Rusty drew out the word. "In a lovely Marsala sauce, as they nestle in a bed of wild rice."

"Sounds good."

"I can give you the phone number—"

"Rusty!" Agnes immediately moderated her voice. "As long as Trent is here, perhaps he could wrestle that heavy old ham out of the oven for us."

"Certainly, Mrs. Romero."

As Trent crossed the kitchen, Rusty mimicked, "Certainly, Mrs. Romero," behind his back.

Her grandmother glared.

Trent removed the ham. "I guess this means we'll be eating soon? I need to make a couple of telephone calls and wanted to check your timetable."

"Dinner will be served soon," Agnes trilled. "But please, do take your time. The ham should sit for a few minutes anyway."

Rusty would have mimicked her grandmother, too, but she wasn't that brave.

Trent's remark reminded Rusty that she needed to make a couple of calls to see how things had gone in the office today, too. Looking around the mess in the kitchen, she knew it would be several hours before she could steal away to find a telephone with some privacy.

"What were you so hot about when I came in here just now?" Trent asked as Rusty's grandmother carried the cornbread and salad into the dining room.

"Gran was wondering when we should put chicken on the menu. She mentioned seeing some running around outside."

"Not those!" Trent blanched. "Those are Cochin chickens, Doc's pride and joy. He raises them for show."

"You mean, they're like pets?" This was great. They wouldn't be expected to cook pets.

"Very special pets. If you want chickens to eat, check the deep-freeze." He opened the walk-in pantry door and flipped on the light. At the back sat a large white chest. "Doc experiments with special feed and food supplements on several different animals. It's his hobby now that he's sold his veterinary practice."

"Good. I'll tell Gran to bury the hatchet—so to speak."

Trent chuckled and lifted the heavy freezer lid. White vapors clouded the top. Waving them away, Trent revealed a well-stocked freezer.

Rusty sighed in relief. That was more like it. She stepped inside the pantry, then stopped. "Look at all this stuff!" She pulled out a box of tissue-wrapped grapefruit. Each one was an unblemished yellow. "Are these real?"

Trent nodded. "Fruit of the Month Club. Each of my uncles belongs to a different one. Uncle Harvey may belong to several."

"No kidding. Can we eat these?"

"Yes, in fact, he was concerned about some pears that came several days ago. He thought they weren't ripe."

Trent peered into several decorative crates and boxes. "Here they are." He carried a domed bowl into the kitchen. "This is a fruit ripener," he explained.

"Of course it is." And from the appearance of the pears, it worked quite well. "I think we'll have these for dinner." She hefted one glorious pear in each hand.

"It looks like you've got everything under control. Call me when you're ready to serve dinner." Trent's gaze flicked down to her Kiss-the-Cook-emblazoned chest. He stared for a moment, then said, "I'll take a rain check." Grinning, he left the kitchen.

Rusty hated aprons, especially aprons that invited smart-aleck remarks from dictatorial ranchers.

DINNER PROVED TO BE ... interesting. Trent found the food uninspired but tolerable—except for the green bean mess. Weren't the onion rings supposed to be crispy?

But he shouldn't be too quick to judge since the women had only just arrived.

And his uncles seemed satisfied. Yet Trent didn't want them becoming too satisfied. He could only spare a few more days on their find-Trent-a-wife project.

"Yes, I've found the Worthington hams to be superior. They trim to leave only the smallest layer of fat before baking." Harvey helped himself to another slice.

"Trent tells us you raise show chickens, Dr. Davis," Agnes said.

"Doc'll do, ma'am." He blotted his mouth with the napkin and proceeded to give a lecture on his prize Cochins.

Normally, Trent would have found a way to shorten the monologue, but Rusty's grandmother was listening with apparent interest. And with Doc talking, Trent didn't have to come up with anything to say. He looked across the table to see Rusty's reaction.

Rusty was staring at her plate.

Her hair was a pretty color in the subdued lighting of the dining room. Not quite red, yet more than a plain brown, it was definitely the rust color of her nickname.

She wasn't at all the sort of person Trent had expected to answer his uncles' profile. From the little they'd spoken, Trent knew she definitely had strong opinions that she wasn't afraid to express and seemed a modern sort of city girl. So what appealed to her about living on the Triple D?

The rat race must have gotten to her. Two couples Trent knew had quit their jobs, sold everything, moved into the country and home-schooled their children. They called it "simplifying their lives." Another couple was considering it.

Trent couldn't understand them. Didn't they get bored?

He studied Rusty's downcast head.

She flinched, then glared at her grandmother.

"*Isn't* the house lovely, dear?" Agnes prompted.

"Yes." Trent could see Rusty gather herself. "I love the fireplace. I hope the weather turns cold enough to have a fire," she said.

And Trent suddenly visualized her in front of the fireplace, the golden glow turning her hair into molten copper.

No. Wrong. Dangerous image. He liked blondes with a yen for honeymoons and an allergy to weddings.

He cleared his throat. "There's plenty of wood out back. Any time you want a fire, just grab an ax."

"Now, boy," his uncle Clarence warned.

Trent didn't listen because he knew what Clarence was about to say.

However, Rusty...Rusty slowly turned her head and raised an eyebrow. That disdainful arch said it all. Trent knew exactly what she thought of his comment and of him for making it. She remained silent because of his uncles and her grandmother.

This was almost too easy. At this rate Rusty and her grandmother would be gone by the end of the weekend and Trent could hasten their departure without his uncles ever knowing exactly what he'd done.

Trent succumbed to the urge to bait Rusty. "That was a mighty fine supper," he said, patting his stomach. "Though dessert demonstrates a woman's true cooking talent, and I know you've been—" What was Clarence's phrase? "Cooking up a storm in there to impress me."

The other eyebrow arched to join the first.

"So what's for dessert?" Trent was enjoying himself.

"Brownies and chocolate chip cookies," Agnes supplied when her granddaughter remained silent. "It was Rusty's suggestion."

"My favorite," Trent said. If he could have belched on command, he would have done so.

"Which one?" Rusty asked.

"I like 'em both so much, I think we ought to have them at every meal." He grinned wolfishly.

From the look on her face, he knew that brownies and chocolate chip cookies would not make another appearance at the Triple D table while she was here.

Too bad. He did like brownies.

"It's time to clear the table," Agnes prompted Rusty. "Would anyone like coffee?"

Everyone murmured their assent and the two women took away the dishes.

As soon as Rusty disappeared with the last plate, Clarence began speaking. "Trent, you are doing nothing to fix that girl's interest."

"I've been talking to her," Trent protested.

"Not the way you talked to Miranda," Harvey countered.

He shouldn't underestimate Harvey's powers of observation, Trent reminded himself. "She's different than Miranda."

Doc nodded. "Wider pelvis and a bit stockier. Doesn't have the shoulders, but you do. Looks strong and has good teeth. And you can tell by the grandmother that she's from a good bloodline."

"Don't be too quick to judge by this dinner, Trent. I know you like your fancy food, but this is wholesome farm food and never hurt a body." Clarence patted his stomach the way Trent had earlier.

"She'll want romance, Trent. Flowers—I've got several catalogs and when the time is right—" Harvey glanced toward the kitchen door and lowered his voice "—I've got a new Victoria's Secret catalog."

"You didn't tell us the new one came." Clarence sounded aggrieved.

"I know how to court a woman," Trent broke in when he could. "I just haven't decided if this is one I wish to court."

The three Davis brothers opened their mouths to protest just as Agnes entered, carrying a tray of coffee cups.

From then on, Trent was prompted, usually by a nudge from Harvey's sneaker-clad foot, into engaging Rusty in conversation.

"Tell me how you managed to come across the issue of *Texas Men*," Trent said as his opening gambit.

Rusty flinched, glanced briefly at her grandmother, and then met Trent's eyes. "Someone brought it to the office."

Harvey leaned forward eagerly. "And when you saw Trent's picture you knew he was the one, right?"

"I knew he was something, all right," Rusty agreed.

"Ow." Harvey frowned at Clarence.

A rustling sounded and Rusty glared at her grandmother.

"You said you work in Dallas but you want to give up your job and move here, is that right?" Rusty's expression was pleasant, but strained.

"No, I—"

Harvey's foot connected with his shin.

"Eventually." Trent leveled a look at Harvey.

"What exactly do you do?"

"I manage investments and assemble financing packages."

"He takes good care of us," Harvey said.

Interest appeared in Rusty's eyes.

Great, thought Trent. Mention money and they're all interested.

"So what kind of deals do you have cooking now?" Rusty swiveled, presumably out of her grandmother's reach.

"Now, Rusty, dear, this business talk is all so complicated."

"But I want to hear—"

"Why don't we just enjoy our coffee. Cookie, Trent? Rusty baked these herself."

"Gran!"

Trent took one and bit into it. "Very good." Burned on the bottom.

Agnes tittered. "I tried to help her and left some in the oven a wee bit too long."

"But, Gran, I didn't—"

"Rusty, the gentlemen need their coffee warmed." Agnes smiled around the table. "Now, Doc, do you only show chickens, or are there other prize-winning animals here on the ranch?"

Rusty glowered and left the room.

"Trent." Harvey rubbed his arms. "I'm cold."

Pushing back his chair, Trent stood. "I'll adjust the thermostat."

"*Trent*, I'm *cold*." Harvey raised his eyebrows and jerked his head toward the fireplace. "I imagine Miss Rusty and Miss Agnes are cold, too."

The fireplace yawned blackly. Harvey wanted a fire and he wanted a fire because Rusty had mentioned it.

"Then a fire is just what we need to take the chill off," Trent offered with false cheer.

Harvey smiled happily.

"How lovely," said Agnes.

Trudging toward the kitchen, Trent walked through the doorway in time to see Rusty bang the cappuccino machine with her fist.

"What are you doing?"

She whirled around, guilt written on her features. "Eventually, I hope to extract coffee from this machine."

"That'll teach you to play hooky during the demo." Trent checked to see that she'd loaded the coffee grounds properly. After reseating the basket, he flipped a switch and within moments a hissing sound announced the arrival of hot water.

"Thanks," she said. "Where are you going?"

"To split some logs for firewood. Harvey thought you might be cold."

A delighted grin spread over her face. "Oh, I am." She stamped her feet and rubbed her hands together. "Brrr. I'm freezing."

Trent slipped his jacket off the peg by the back door. "Somehow, I thought you would be."

"You're not angry, are you, Trent? This is man's work, just the way you wanted it. You remember, men providing, women nurturing?" She smiled smugly.

"Ah, yes, nurturing." He paused, his hand on the doorknob. "I can guarantee that when I finish splitting those logs for your fire, I'm going to need serious nurturing—and I'll expect more than burned chocolate chip cookies."

Before he went out the door, Trent had the satisfaction of watching Rusty Romero's smug smile disappear.

4

"RUSTY, wake up."

Rusty opened her eyes to find her grandmother standing over her in the gray predawn light. "What's the matter?"

"You've got to hurry and get into the kitchen."

Dragging herself into a sitting position, Rusty tried to wake up. "You smell like bacon."

"Things got a trifle smoky."

"Nothing's on fire, is it?"

Her grandmother shook her head, "Nothing important."

"Then I'll just go back to sleep." Rusty slid down the headboard.

"No, you have to get dressed." Agnes rummaged through the pile of clothes on the chair. "There isn't much time."

"Are we sneaking away?" Rusty threw aside the covers. The day was shaping up nicely after all.

"This *can't* be your robe." Agnes held out a velour robe with velourless patches at the elbows.

"I promise not to wear it on the plane." Rusty tied her favorite garment around her.

"We're not leaving. I want you to get dressed in something pretty. Did you bring pink?"

"Pink?" Rusty made a gagging motion.

"Yes." Agnes pushed Rusty's bangs off her forehead and examined her. "It'll complement that rosy color in your eyes."

"If you'd let me go back to sleep, that rosy color will go away."

Agnes was unsympathetic. "If you hadn't stayed awake so long last night, you wouldn't be sleepy this morning."

Rusty yawned. "I had work to do and we didn't get out of that kitchen until ten-thirty. Did you have to offer them bedtime snacks?"

"It was the least we could do after dear Trent chopped all that wood."

Dear Trent had been moving kind of slow after hauling in the firewood last night, Rusty remembered. She smiled. It almost made her forget that her own back was sore from standing up so long. How could her grandmother function so early in the morning?

Agnes was pushing Rusty toward the bathroom. "Put on your makeup and hurry out to the kitchen. Breakfast is nearly ready."

"You've already cooked breakfast?" The thought of food so early was definitely unappetizing.

"The men eat early and often here in the country," Agnes informed her.

"I would've helped you," Rusty grumbled. Or tried to talk her into waiting an hour.

"It doesn't matter now. Hurry, or you'll spoil everything." Agnes gave her a final push.

It was more the thought of a mug of coffee than her grandmother's urging that sent Rusty shuffling out to the kitchen after throwing on jeans and a baggy sweater.

"Rusty, couldn't you have put on some lipstick?" Agnes asked when she saw her. "Well, never mind. Trent probably prefers the wholesome country girl look."

Rusty did an about-face. "I've got some Chanel Vamp in my purse."

"Not that ghastly color." Agnes grabbed her arm. "Halloween was weeks ago, dear."

Then why were they masquerading as happy homemakers? Rusty wondered. "Is the coffee ready?"

"Not yet. We want it to be fresh."

"Don't worry. The first pot's for me." With single-minded determination, Rusty headed for the cappuccino machine. She wanted plain, unadorned coffee. That shouldn't be too much to ask, should it?

Tiny vacuumed-packed foil pouches of various flavored coffees stood at attention in the cabinet above the machine. "I had no idea there were coffee bean clubs. Oh, hazelnut crème." Flavored coffee suddenly sounded just right.

She put the machine on Drip and turned around, blinking as the condition of the kitchen finally registered. "How much food did you cook?"

Agnes hurried over. "Here put this on."

"Oh, Gran, not the cow apron."

"You'll look cute in it."

Rusty winced at the word "cute." Her grandmother pulled her arms through as though she were a little girl, spun her around and tied the apron behind her back. "Bulky over that sweater, but functional. Hold this."

Rusty found herself with a spatula in her hand as her grandmother propelled her toward the stove.

Something was burning.

"Drat and double drat." Agnes jerked the skillet off the stove and dumped out the contents. "This is a gas stove and the one in my apartment is an electric one."

Rusty followed her over to the sink and noticed several other burnt offerings. "Pancakes?"

"It's awful." Agnes sounded desperate. "There's hardly any batter left. You try to cook one." The oven timer buzzed and she hurried off.

Rusty dipped batter into the iron skillet. It hissed and smoked. She turned the flame lower.

"At least these came out." Agnes carried a pan of biscuits to the butcher block. They joined bacon, sausage and ham.

"Gran . . . that's a lot of food. Who's going to eat it all?"

"Appetites are bigger on the farm."

Farm. Her grandmother must be reliving her girlhood when she and the other women had had to cook for all the farm workers. Though how she could mistake the three egg-shaped Davis brothers for lean cowhands was beyond Rusty.

She decided not to say anything more. Her grandmother obviously felt a huge breakfast was called for on their first morning. Fine. They'd have a huge breakfast and then see who ate what and how much. Tomorrow, there'd be changes.

Sneaking across the kitchen, Rusty maneuvered a mug under the still-brewing coffee and only splashed a little getting the pot back onto the burner.

Agnes looked up at the hissing sound. "Rusty! You abandoned your post."

"A momentary lapse, ma'am." Saluting, Rusty returned to the stove and tried to flip her pancake. It was burnt on the bottom and runny on the top. She tried turning it anyway, but it fell apart. Eventually, she scraped the mess into the sink.

Agnes sighed. "I've put toast in the oven to broil since we apparently won't be having many pancakes."

"Toast? You've got biscuits."

"Someone might want toast. Be sure and watch it. And I've put out eggs. Ask them how they want their eggs cooked."

"There's more than one way?"

"Rusty, *try* and cooperate!" Agnes hurried from the room.

"Where are you going?" Rusty called, but didn't get a response.

Toast was ridiculous and she couldn't do two things at once. Rusty turned off the broiler and concentrated on her next pancake attempt. Eggs. Nobody should be eating eggs. And if they did, Rusty would scramble them because that's the only way she knew how to fix them.

There was a pot on the stove. Peering into it, Rusty saw a lumpy gray mass. Oatmeal. She poked it with a wooden spoon. The spoon bounced off the surface, so she stabbed it. The spoon stood at attention. No oatmeal today.

"Poor Gran." Shaking her head, Rusty sipped at her coffee and checked the bottom of the pancake.

"Well, good morning!" Trent's uncle Clarence poked his head into the kitchen. "What have we here?"

Rusty straightened. "Breakfast."

"So I see—and smell." Closing his eyes, Clarence inhaled. "Biscuits." He wandered over to the butcher block. "My Emma made the best biscuits."

"Good morning!"

At her grandmother's voice, Rusty turned, then stared.

Agnes, her hair mussed, was dressed in a robe—and not one of her satin peignoirs, either. This was a quilted yellow print. Calico. Her grandmother was wearing calico.

"I must have overslept. Rusty, you should have called me." Agnes gave her open-mouthed granddaughter a hug.

"What are you doing?" Rusty whispered. "You look like an extra in a spaghetti Western."

"Flip your pancake," Agnes replied, and wandered over to marvel at the bounty on the butcher block, as though seeing the food for the first time.

Obviously, she intended for her granddaughter to get sole credit for the morning meal. Rusty toyed with the idea of exposing her grandmother and would have, if Trent hadn't chosen that moment to walk in. "Now this is a serious breakfast." He met her eyes. "I'm impressed."

Her grandmother shot her a triumphant look to which Rusty responded by flipping her pancake with a resounding splat. To her utter surprise, the top was a golden brown. "Oh! Gran, come look!"

Agnes rushed over. "Don't act so surprised," she whispered. "They're always supposed to look like that." In a louder voice, she sang, "Anyone want eggs?"

"Two, sunny-side up," Trent said on his way to the coffeepot.

Rusty glared after him. "That would be the unbroken kind, right?"

Agnes laughed shrilly. "Oh, Rusty, such a sense of humor. Do you like a woman with a sense of humor in the mornings, Trent?"

His eyes gleamed. "Occasionally."

Rusty took in his unshaven face—and the fact that he'd emptied the coffeepot. "He probably has to take what he can get."

Trent saluted her with his coffee mug.

Just then Doc and Harvey came in through the back door. Their entry provided sufficient distraction for Agnes to break the eggs into a small skillet without anyone noticing. The yolks remained whole.

"How'd you do that?" Rusty murmured.

Doc stopped short when he saw Agnes at the stove. His gaze went from Agnes to Rusty, then back to Agnes, whose cheeks were pink.

"Did you feed all your animals?" she asked, not meeting his eyes.

"Yes, ma'am." Nodding, he passed by them.

"I encountered Doc this morning when I came to the kitchen for...something to drink," Agnes explained to Rusty in tones loud enough for everyone to hear. "I didn't expect to find anyone out and about so early." She finished with a forced chuckle.

I'll bet you didn't. Her grandmother was blushing. A good thing, too. She needed the color to counteract the yellow calico.

Rusty wondered just how much of her grandmother's activities good old Doc had witnessed in the kitchen.

"Did the Back-Saver 92A sleep good?" Clarence grabbed a biscuit as Harvey wandered by.

"Not as superior as the 92B model, but I need two more nights on it for an accurate comparison." Deep in thought, Harvey was oblivious to the food.

"Breakfast is ready," Clarence informed him. "Don't spend too long making notes."

"I won't," was the vague response as Harvey drifted from the room.

Doc followed him, making a muttered remark about cleaning up.

Silence followed as Clarence snitched another biscuit and Agnes stared at the eggs.

"Coffee's all gone," Trent told Rusty.

"I can *see* that," she snapped.

Agnes poked her. "I can watch Trent's eggs while you make more coffee."

Couldn't he make his own coffee? For her grandmother's sake, Rusty swallowed her annoyance and made another pot. Trent watched her measure the grounds, then set his empty mug beside the pot. "I'll be in the dining room."

Where he obviously expected to be served, Rusty fumed. Imagine waking up to this work every morning for the rest of her life.

Forget it. She'd stay single.

Rusty spent the next hour carrying plates in and out of the dining room, refilling coffee, juice and milk, and rewarming meats that had gone cold because they'd been cooked too far in advance.

Agnes, her color heightened, frantically made more pancake batter when Rusty's lonely pancake was praised by Harvey. Rusty's "Let them eat toast" comment had no effect, especially since she'd turned off the broiler before toasting the other side of the bread.

Trent read the *Wall Street Journal* and ate his food without comment, leaving before Rusty even sat down. She found she was so resentful she couldn't eat, so she excused herself to do the dishes, leaving an exhausted Agnes drinking coffee with the uncles.

Trent had some nerve. Her grandmother must have spent hours cooking. In fact, as soon as the uncles went off to do whatever they did, Rusty would insist that Agnes go back to bed. The uncles, especially Clarence, had been highly complimentary. Trent had barely said a word. Would a little praise kill him?

Rusty loaded the dishwasher, but there were so many dishes left over, she resigned herself to washing the rest by hand.

She wrestled with the heavy cast-iron skillets, scrubbing them with steel wool. It was taking forever and she was desperate to hook up her modem and contact her office. Her assistant, Alisa, had express instructions to E-mail Rusty daily with any news of her competition for the campaign. She sighed, wishing she could be at the office to oversee the final details of her presentation. She couldn't believe she was scrubbing pots and pans while the opportunity of her professional life was within grasp.

"Any more coffee?" A freshly shaven Trent padded across the black-and-white tiled floor.

"Whatever's left in the pot," Rusty said through gritted teeth. Because of him, she was hundreds of miles from home instead of fine-tuning her advertising campaign. And he didn't even seem to appreciate her efforts, well technically, her grandmother's efforts, but still.

"There's a little." He emptied the rest into his mug and looked at her questioningly.

"Why, yes, thank you. I *would* like some." Forearm-deep in sudsy water, Rusty pushed her bangs out of her eyes with her shoulder.

Trent stood there, holding the empty pot in one hand and his mug in the other. "There wasn't much left."

"Well, the coffee fairy is busy, so I guess you'll have to make more," Rusty snapped.

"I didn't realize you wanted coffee." Trent spoke very carefully, which only angered Rusty more. "I thought you were ready to wash the pot."

Of course. "Sure, just add it to the mountain of dirty dishes over there."

"I can make more coffee—"

"Can you?"

Trent's lips pressed together. "What is the matter with you?"

Rusty was mad and her grandmother wasn't in the room to stop her from saying what she felt. "You sat at that table, read a newspaper and ate without saying a word. Don't you have any idea how long it took to fix all that food?" Rusty conveniently ignored the fact that she didn't have any idea, either.

Trent set the coffeepot down. "The food was great." He hesitated. "But I'm not really a big breakfast person. Dry cereal would have been fine."

It was all Rusty could do to keep from using the skillet as a weapon. He could have told them. "Dry cereal? What happened to 'cook up a storm and hang the cholesterol'?"

"What?" He appeared genuinely puzzled.

"Your profile in *Texas Men*."

"Oh, that."

"Yes, *that*."

"Well . . ." Trent rubbed his forehead. "I guess I was tired of dry cereal then." He offered a smile.

They stared at each other for a few seconds.

Trent looked away first. "I think we have a plain old drip coffee maker somewhere around here." He started opening and closing cabinet doors. "It's got a bigger pot so you won't have to remake coffee so often." He pulled out a white model just like the one Rusty had in her apartment and set it on the counter. "I'll make a pot as soon as I find the filters," he offered.

"Don't bother. I don't really want any more coffee." Rusty rinsed the skillet and set it on the sideboard.

Trent stood there a moment longer. "Okay, then I guess I'll see you at lunch." With a brief, impersonal smile, he left Rusty to her dishes.

He could have offered to dry, she grumbled to herself. At this rate, when she finished, it would be time to start fixing lunch.

She banged another skillet into the sink. Dry cereal. That was unexpected. In fact, come to think of it, Trent's behavior was unexpected. The only time he'd paid any attention to her was at his uncles' urging. He hardly seemed to be checking her out as a potential helpmate and nurturer.

Rusty brightened. Maybe she'd already flunked his wife test.

HE DID NOT understand this woman. If he'd known she'd wanted the dregs of the coffee, he would have made himself a cup of instant.

She certainly didn't have a sweetly compliant disposition and he ought to be relieved that she wasn't the clingy type. He'd get more work done and he didn't want to endear himself to her, since there was no future for her here.

But she wasn't trying to attract him *at all*.

Honestly, it appeared as though she'd just rolled out of bed. The back of her hair was fluffed up from where she'd slept on it. Having seen her yesterday, Trent knew Rusty wasn't wearing makeup to enhance those brown eyes, so her brows must be naturally dark. She was swimming in a baggy sweater with a neckline that had a tendency to shift to the right, revealing a beige, lace-free bra strap.

She actually looked kind of cute, in a slovenly sort of way. He hadn't realized before that slovenly could look cute. Obviously, he'd been dating too many blond fashion plates.

And her attitude was so prickly, especially about breakfast. He supposed he should have raved over the food, but frankly, the sausage was cold, the biscuits weren't warm enough to melt the butter and the eggs were overdone.

He probably should have said something anyway. Maybe that *was* the reason for her antagonism. He'd be sure and praise her efforts at lunch so she'd feel appreciated.

But not encouraged. The last thing he wanted to do was offer any encouragement to Rusty Romero and her grandmother. But it was becoming increasingly difficult to tread the line between rudeness and indifference.

Sighing to himself, Trent sat in front of his computer. All the bids for building supplies were coming in and he would have to select one prior to the end of the year. It meant keeping abreast of the price of the raw materials along with a hundred other details.

Dialing the number of a stock quote service, he waited for his modem to connect. Nothing. Picking up the phone, he heard Harvey ordering fresh balsam fir wreaths.

Quietly replacing the phone, Trent took a long, slow breath. How was he going to get anything done?

RUSTY FIGURED she had half an hour of free time before she had to start preparing lunch. The dishes were dried and put away, Agnes was resting, the three men were parked in their loungers in front of the big-screen TV and Trent was who knew—and who cared—where. She could check her E-mail.

All she needed was a phone jack. Neither bedroom had a telephone, so she slipped down the hall, carrying her laptop with her. She passed the master suite, where King Trent was probably ensconced, and kept going. At the end of the hall, she saw a closed door. Another bedroom. She tapped, and when there was no answer, she opened the door.

Trent sat in front of a computer, holding his head in his hands. He looked up before Rusty could retreat.

"I, uh, sorry."

"Did you need something?" His look was wary.

He probably thought she was tracking him down in his lair. What an ego.

"A telephone outlet."

His gaze dropped to the laptop in her arms.

"I . . . wanted to check my E-mail." Frankly, at this point, Rusty didn't care what Trent thought about her or the type of woman she was supposed to be. She was desperate to contact her office.

Trent leaned his head back and stared at the ceiling. "There's a jack in here, but Harvey is tying up the line. Even if you could get through, he constantly picks up and breaks the connection."

"Oh." Curious, Rusty wandered further into the room. "What are you doing?"

Without lifting his head from the back of the chair, he turned and looked at her. "A project with an end-of-the-year timeline."

"I hear that." Rusty sat on a trunk at the foot of the bed. "Would your Uncle Harvey mind if we just asked to use the phone?"

"Probably not for you, but I'm supposed to be on vacation. He'd lecture me about not relaxing." Trent sighed and got to his feet. "Tell you what, I'll go distract him and you can get, oh, maybe, five minutes of phone time. Will that help?"

"Yes." Rusty hesitated, then offered, "Maybe I can do the same for you."

Trent smiled. "Deal."

He could really be quite attractive, Rusty thought, watching Trent walk from the room. The rear view wasn't bad, either.

And he didn't seem to be the slightest bit interested in her.

Earlier, when she'd thought that, she'd been satisfied. Things could have become so sticky and awkward when she'd be forced to tell him that her future was not on some ranch. He would have been devastated, naturally, because he was unlikely to see a woman of Rusty's caliber answering his silly ad, if she did say so herself.

Now she wasn't so sure. Having an attractive and relationship-free man express complete disinterest was not good for her feminine ego. She'd think about that some other time. Right now, she had to connect her computer.

Trent was as good as his word and within moments Rusty had retrieved her E-mail and captured it in a file to read later. She didn't want to chance taking up too much time.

With a few minutes left before Trent's return, Rusty checked out his setup. He had a nifty laser printer—better than the portable inkjet she'd brought. Maybe he'd let her use it. Her laptop was better than his computer, though, she noticed with satisfaction.

Next to the bed, against the wall, were boxes of papers and file folders. Good grief, it looked like the man had brought his entire office. He obviously hadn't intended to take any sort of vacation. Now, that didn't matter to her, but hadn't he planned to spend any time getting to know the woman who'd responded to his *Texas Men* profile? Or perhaps he hadn't anticipated such a heavy end-of-the-year workload when he'd sent in his ad.

"See anything you like?" Trent walked through the doorway, his expression stern.

"Yeah, your laser printer." Rusty hooked a thumb over her shoulder. "Mind if I borrow it sometime?"

He gazed at her, unblinking. "You've got nerve, I'll give you that."

"Why?"

"I do you a favor, catch you snooping through my stuff, and you ask to borrow my printer." He advanced until he was close enough to invade her personal space.

Rusty kind of liked having him stand so close. Little prickles of awareness raised the hairs on the back of her neck. "Hey, if I were snooping, you'd never know it. By the way, thanks for the phone time."

"No problem." Still stern-faced, he hadn't moved.

A power play. Well, *she* wasn't going to yield. In fact...Rusty looked up at him and leaned a fraction of an inch closer to increase the stakes. He retained his position, though something flashed deep in the back of those chocolate brown eyes.

Just to see what would happen, Rusty sent him one of those if-you-try-and-kiss-me-I-might-just-let-you looks.

His eyes narrowed. Obviously he knew the look. His gaze darted around the room and Rusty could almost hear his internal male alarm sound. *Warning. You are alone in a bedroom with a marriageable female. Proceed with caution.*

Holding up a finger, Trent said, "I don't know what your game is, but I don't want to play." Taking her shoulders and spinning her around, he walked her to the door.

She'd gotten to him. He'd tried to intimidate her and hadn't. Rusty felt daring. "Why do you think it's a game?"

"Life is a game."

"And all the men and women merely players. Playing sounds like fun, huh?"

"Not to me."

Rusty turned around in the doorway and stopped so he ran into her. "Well, it does to me."

He looked down at her. "That's exactly what I'm afraid of." A pulse throbbed in his temple.

"Afraid?" Rusty held their chest-to-chest position.

He didn't blink. "Uninterested."

She raised her eyebrow. "Uninterested in women in general?"

His gaze left her eyes and swept the length of her. "You in particular."

Ouch. She'd given him the opening, but hadn't expected him to use it so effectively. Teasing him had lost its allure. She backed off.

If he wasn't interested, he wasn't interested. Fine. His loss. His sort didn't appeal to her anyway. "Okay, I understand," she said with forced cheerfulness, stepping backward into the hall.

With a clear conscience, Rusty could now report to her grandmother that Trent was off the list and her matchmaking should cease at once. In fact, there was no reason for them to remain at the Triple D. They could go home. Soon. It had been a productive morning.

"See you at lunch." She smiled, unable to resist one last shot. "No hard feelings—so to speak."

Rusty had already turned to leave. In one movement Trent grabbed her arm and hauled her against him.

"Wha—"

Cupping her head with his hand, he swooped down and captured her open mouth with his.

Shock held her immobile as Trent demonstrated that he was one of the world's all time great kissers. Absolutely masterful, yet at no time did she feel the slightest bit threatened. Instinctively, Rusty knew that at the first sign of resistance, Trent would release her.

So she was careful not to resist.

Unfortunately, before she could actively participate, he broke the kiss. For a few more seconds his lips remained just an inch above hers as he gazed into her eyes.

"*Now* you can leave," he said, releasing her.

And then he shut the door.

5

THAT WAS NOT uninterested. That was definitely interested. Even though he'd just been responding to that crack she'd made, there was definite interest in that kiss.

Rusty stared at the closed door for longer than she would have liked. She didn't want to admit that she half hoped—okay, fully hoped—Trent would open the door and kiss her again. A girl didn't encounter Olympic gold medal kissers often enough to ignore one when she did.

Alas, the door remained closed.

Perhaps she ought to rethink her timetable for leaving the Triple D, Rusty reflected as she took a step and found that her knees wobbled.

HEAD PRESSING on the closed door, Trent held his breath until he heard Rusty's footfalls retreat down the hallway.

What had he been thinking? Well, he knew what he'd been thinking, but *how* could he have thought it? Or done it?

He deliberately bumped his forehead against the doorjamb. *Stupid, stupid.*

Prior to this little slip, he'd done everything but hang a sign saying, I'm Not Interested. He'd even told her he wasn't interested. Then he had to go and kiss her, which she'd interpret as him being interested.

And he was, but not in the whole marriage scenario that came with her. Unfortunately, marriage was the ultimate purpose of her visit here. She'd brought her *grandmother*, for pity's sake. How much more proper could she get? And she expected him to be looking for a wife to live with him on the ranch. Trent wasn't ready to live on the ranch yet, so he couldn't, in good conscience, encourage her. Or take advantage of her.

True, she'd been surprisingly aggressive. True, he'd liked it. But he was supposed to be discouraging her, and now any hope of Rusty Romero and her grandmother throwing in the towel and leaving the Triple D early was gone. He'd given her hope.

A marriage-minded woman with hope was a formidable opponent.

Like Clarence on one of his bad days, Trent slowly made his way across the room to the computer, slumped onto the chair and stared at the screen. The situation was not unsalvageable *if* he exhibited no further interest in her, which meant remaining cordially remote and no kissing.

Trent thought again of her mouth and the pleasantly stunned look on her face, the teasing look in her eyes . . . how she'd felt in his arms . . . the way she insisted on making each meeting a confrontation . . . and the way he was beginning to look forward to those meetings . . .

Showing complete apathy toward Rusty Romero was going to be harder than he thought.

IT WAS A TESTAMENT to Trent's kissing expertise that
Rusty dropped off her laptop and headed for the
kitchen without reading her E-mail. By the time she remembered, she and Agnes were in the middle of making soup and sandwiches.

"We'll have a light lunch and cook something special
for supper," Agnes said. She had dressed and when
Rusty had wandered, dazed, through the den with the
loungers and big-screen TV, she'd been chatting happily with the uncles. "We're planning decorations for
the house. And tomorrow, we'll cut down a Christmas
tree! Can you imagine?"

"Sounds like fun." Sounded like work, but her
grandmother was so excited, Rusty tried to muster
some enthusiasm.

"This afternoon, we can look for cookie recipes and
try one."

She'd better grab some time for herself before her
entire stay was planned. "Uh, Gran? I may have to let
you choose the recipe. There was a message from Alisa
that I haven't had time to read yet."

"But how will I know what cookies appeal to you?"

Slathering mayonnaise on bread, Rusty thought
quickly. "We've never had time to make those really
fancy Christmas cookies. You know, the decorated
kind? How about those?"

Agnes beamed. "That'll be so much fun!"

And time-consuming. While her grandmother fooled
around with all that colored icing, Rusty should have
hours to herself.

By the time lunch was ready, Rusty had decided that
she would treat Trent very matter-of-factly. After all,

nothing had really changed, she told herself. She'd teased him and he'd called her bluff. The balance of power was equal once more.

As long as Trent kept his lips to himself.

So when he beckoned to her right before they sat down to eat, Rusty took her time before responding. "Did you retrieve your E-mail okay?" he asked under his breath.

Apparently, Rusty wasn't the only one to decide that it was business as usual. How unfortunate for her peace of mind that it took this query from Trent to remind her that she hadn't even read Alisa's message.

"Yes. In fact, I need to act on it."

"If Harvey's eating, he isn't dialing," Trent commented, sitting in his seat.

Rusty took the hint, scarfed down her sandwich and escaped from the table, ignoring Agnes's raised eyebrows.

There were three separate messages from Alisa, which immediately alarmed Rusty. The first one assured her that all was well. The second mentioned that George Kaylee, Rusty's chief rival for the Next to Nature campaign bid, was also out of the office for the rest of the week. Rusty breathed a little easier. Maybe since she was gone, he'd also decided to take a break from the long hours that pulling together an ad campaign demanded.

But the third message made Rusty queasy. Alisa reported that she'd run into George's assistant in the supply room where she'd requisitioned materials for mounting photos. *Mounting photos?*

Rusty had a bad feeling about that. George was spending all his time on his Next to Nature presentation, as was she, so why did he need to mount photos? She'd planned to illustrate storyboards with sketches and knew George was doing so, as well. That was the way they worked. Cost prohibited them from hiring models and photographers for an in-house proposal—unless George was paying for a professional shoot out of his own pocket. Which he very well could be.

After typing a message imploring Alisa to find out what was going on, Rusty raced into Trent's room and sent the E-mail.

He arrived just as she was hooking the phone line back to his computer.

"Hey, are you coming or going?"

"Going." Rusty got to her feet, her thoughts back in Chicago. What was George up to? She should *be* there at this crucial time to keep an eye on him and her own project. Sighing, she closed her laptop.

"Bad news?" Trent asked.

She'd forgotten he was standing there.

"I don't know yet." Rusty frowned, then remembered she owed Trent some free phone time. "Do you need me to stall Harvey for you?" She looked directly at him for the first time since he'd entered the room.

Mistake. Trent was staring at her mouth.

"Hmm?"

She wished he wouldn't do that. "Phone time?"

He drew a deep breath. "Yeah." His gaze left her mouth and met her eyes.

They gazed at each other. Rusty knew what *she* was thinking and had a fairly good idea that Trent was thinking the same thing. He was remembering kissing her. And she was remembering being kissed.

And neither one of them planned to act on those memories.

Trent stood aside and Rusty walked past, holding herself carefully so she wouldn't touch him.

She made it all the way to the door before Trent spoke.

"If you can, give me some notice when you plan to pry my uncles away from the telephone."

"Gran said something about cookies." Rusty paused in the doorway. "I bet we'll have a midafternoon snack. In fact, I'll suggest it. That would be a good time."

Trent grinned. "Thanks."

Rusty then proceeded to spend all afternoon in the kitchen trying to learn enough to fake a lifetime of baking expertise. So much for free time. Well, she really couldn't do anything until she heard from Alisa, anyway, and baking cookies with her grandmother was a novel experience.

Mixing up batches of cookie dough wasn't so bad, she found. It almost kept her mind off George's activities.

Periodically, Harvey would gallop into the kitchen and alert Agnes to some product being sold on television. Rusty usually remained in the kitchen and iced cookies while Agnes went to look, but raised voices drew her into the den on one occasion. It was a mistake, because she found herself embroiled in an incident involving lighted pine garland.

"White lights? Have you no imagination, Clarence? Can't you see this room all full of color?" Harvey waved his arms about.

Clarence, the phone to his ear, shushed him.

"Oh, oh!" Harvey hopped up and down and pointed to the screen. "Hand-tied red velvet bows! At only four ninety-nine. It's a steal! A steal, I tell you! And you're on the telephone." He groaned. "Hurry!"

Clarence covered the mouthpiece. "I can order both at the same time, Harvey. How many did you want?"

"You haven't decided on whether you're ordering colored or white lights," declared Doc.

"Colored!" Harvey screeched.

Agnes made ineffective soothing noises. Rusty tried to melt back into the kitchen before her presence registered.

"I won't have the ranch house tarted up—" began Clarence.

"Why don't you let the Romero ladies decide?" suggested a deep voice. Trent walked into the room, crossed his arms and grinned.

Rusty sent him a look of complete disgust. "That's right. Put *us* on the spot."

"The bows, the bows!" Harvey whimpered. "There are only three dozen left!" On the TV screen, in a box announcing the number of items available for purchase, the number of bows declined at an alarming rate, then suddenly dropped to zero.

"Oh, no." Crushed, Harvey collapsed in his recliner. "We'll never see them at that price for that quality ever again."

"White lights or colored lights?" Clarence looked at Agnes.

Agnes looked at Rusty.

Rusty glared at Trent. "White lights, greenery and red velvet bows is one of my favorite looks," she said. "But since we don't have the bows—"

"Oh, we got 'em," Clarence said. "Yes, ma'am," he said into the phone. "That'll be on my American Express card."

"How many?" Harvey clutched the side of the recliner.

Clarence held up two fingers and Harvey's face fell. "*Two?* That's all?"

Clarence shook his head. "Dozen. Give me some credit—no, ma'am, I wasn't speaking to you. You just put the bows and a hundred yards of the *white*-lighted garland on my card."

"Have 'em sent Express Mail service," Doc reminded Clarence.

Clarence nodded.

Closing his eyes, Harvey sighed in relief.

"Harvey, you're missing the cashmere scarves." Doc gestured to the screen. "And look—matching socks."

Harvey sat bolt upright, the contretemps over the lights apparently forgotten. "Cashmere socks sacrifice durability for comfort."

"Your point?" Doc, who had successfully remained neutral during the colored-versus-white-light controversy, was obviously a man who picked his battles.

"Well," Rusty said brightly. "I think we should celebrate with some cocoa and warm cookies." She raised her eyebrows at Trent, who gave her the thumbs-up sign and retreated.

He didn't deserve the favor after putting her in the middle of the light mess, but she *had* promised.

"Rusty, I'm so proud of you," her grandmother whispered. "This is just the sort of afternoon I'd imagined when we decided to come here."

Rather than pointing out that most of their activities had revolved around either the television shopping network or the kitchen, she just hugged her pink-cheeked grandmother.

Rusty turned off the television while the brothers ate cookies and drank cocoa. They didn't seem to miss the TV, turning their attention to the ubiquitous catalogs.

Or most of their attention.

"Trent isn't here," Harvey announced the obvious in the middle of a discussion concerning the taste differences between Texas pecans and Georgia pecans. "And Trent is partial to pecans." The brothers exchanged a look with Agnes.

The natives were getting restless. "I'll get him." Rusty jumped up, grabbing a napkin and two cookies. "Just a sample to lure him out here for more."

Ignoring four satisfied smiles, she hurried down the hall and tapped on Trent's door.

"Come in," he called.

She walked in to find him talking on the telephone. He gestured for her to stay, so she did.

"I'll have it by the thirtieth," he was saying. "That way, we can sign before the end of the business day on the thirty-first."

He sounded so confidently professional he could have been ensconced in a plush executive suite instead of a small back bedroom in a ranch house. This was a man who intended to conduct business, not a man who was trying to catch up on a few things during the holidays.

After a few sign-off pleasantries, he hung up the telephone. "Of course, that was a complete lie on my part." Tension lines creased his forehead.

"Have a cookie." Rusty handed him the napkin, surprised he'd admitted such a thing in front of her.

"And how did you know I needed a cookie?" He gave her a weary smile and bit into a crumbly powdered-sugar-dusted lump.

"The world is a better place when you're eating warm cookies." She wished she'd nabbed a couple for herself.

His dimples appeared briefly. "These are great."

"Aren't they?" Feeling dangerously pleased, Rusty sat on the chest at the foot of the bed again and Trent swiveled in his chair until he faced her. "It's amazing how such a simple cookie can taste so good." Especially when it wasn't burned on the bottom. Harvey's insulated cookie sheets had made all the difference. "We used real butter," she added, in case Trent was avoiding butter. She had no idea what state had provided the pecans.

"Good decision." Trent ate the second cookie.

Rusty grappled with unexpected emotions. Trent's obvious pleasure made her feel warmly satisfied in a feminine, nurturing way. Just the sort of nurturing way she was avoiding. She didn't want to feel as though she'd fulfilled some womanly destiny after waiting on a man. And yet, if Trent had been gruff or unappreciative, she would have been furious. Go figure.

"I didn't get a chance to bring you cocoa," Rusty said. Really, two cookies hardly justified a nesting attack. "Your absence was noted by the group."

"Thanks for the tip." He smiled such an obviously forced smile that Rusty took pity on him. "Problems?"

"Hmm?"

"What are you *not* going to have ready on the thirtieth?" she asked, referring to his earlier comment.

Trent stared at her and Rusty thought she'd never seen such indecision on a man's face before.

He was tempted to talk, yet he was reluctant. Or didn't he feel she was capable of understanding his business woes?

"I don't want to bore you," he said.

"Is that man talk for 'don't worry your little head about it'?" She'd forgotten that he was hung up on separating men's work and women's work.

"It's man talk for once I get started I might not stop." Trent held her gaze in silent rebuke, making Rusty feel ashamed.

"I'm sorry. That was a nasty crack." She pulled her knees to her chest and wrapped her arms around them. "So, what's going on?"

TRENT WANTED to tell her. In fact, he wanted to tell her everything and drop this damn charade.

But he couldn't, and she sat there, ready to listen, looking sincerely interested at a time when he desperately needed feedback from somebody—anybody. Even the nettlesome woman in front of him.

The thing was, he was beginning to like her. He didn't want to like her. He didn't want to think about her at all.

Take the kiss. She could have become all huffy about it, but she'd been a good sport. And he noticed how she'd extended the amused fondness with which she regarded her grandmother to his uncles. She didn't patronize any of them and that counted for a lot in his book.

"A contract," he said, at last answering her question. "I don't think I can have the contract cut by the thirtieth."

"And if you don't?"

Trent brought his fingers together, then opened them wide. "My loan goes poof."

"Is that all? Not that losing a loan isn't enough."

"Actually, no it isn't all. The bids expire, building permits expire, my option on the property I want to buy expires." People's confidence in a Trent not backed by Triple D money would evaporate. He'd probably never get another chance to prove himself.

But he didn't say that to Rusty. He wasn't about to confide *everything* to her.

She was chewing her thumbnail in a classic thoughtful pose. "What's the holdup?"

Only that he was here instead of in Dallas. Only that all the bids were going to his office first before being sent here. Only that he didn't have vital information he needed at his fingertips and had to call his secretary— assuming he could get through. Only that he wished he'd never agreed to his uncles' scheme for meeting a "suitable" woman. But all he said was, "The bids aren't coming in as fast as I'd like."

"What are the bids for?"

Now there was a topic he could discuss without any qualms. "A retirement village. And not one of those places where the elderly just go to wait out their lives. I want a place where they can *live*—with their families nearby, if they want to." He shifted in his chair. "You see, most of these planned communities are family oriented, but they're forgetting the older family members."

He paused to allow her to escape if she wanted to. But he hoped she wouldn't.

"And?" She impatiently gestured with her hand for him to continue.

Pleased, he did. "And since developers have largely ignored this segment of the population, I'm building a community geared for people who've raised their children and are looking forward to an active retirement."

"People have been retiring to these sorts of places in Florida and Arizona for years. How is your plan different?"

Trent was nodding before she finished speaking. "I'm trying to incorporate the whole community, rather than isolate one age group. My plan is to start building the retirement housing and amenities, then add more assisted-living housing, building the houses for families last, since homes for them are more prevalent now. What I really hope is that some other developer will build family housing within the village."

Rusty was gazing at him with a blank look. She was bored. Disappointment stabbed him, the wound deeper than he'd expected. For reasons unknown to him, he'd felt Rusty would be interested. After all, she was obviously close to her grandmother. The time might come when Agnes couldn't live alone anymore.

"You're talking about transition housing, aren't you?"

She'd been paying attention after all. Pleased, he continued, "Not in the traditional sense. Probably a level before that."

Rusty gestured toward the computer and the surrounding debris. "And it all has to come together before the thirtieth?"

Trent nodded.

She eyed him. "You've been very involved with all this since I got here, haven't you?"

He hesitated, nodding again. "Sorry. I lost track of the afternoon." Not to mention the morning.

Rusty and her grandmother were guests here and he'd abandoned them to be entertained by his uncles. He fully expected Clarence to point that out in the very near future along with an admonition to give Rusty a fair chance. It *was* too early to convincingly announce that he and Rusty hadn't hit it off since he hadn't spent any time with her.

True, he'd kissed her, but he'd been annoyed with her when he'd done so. Afterward, he'd been annoyed with himself. He *certainly* didn't think Clarence would be pleased to hear about it.

"Since you're obviously in a time crunch, *why* did you advertise for someone to come and celebrate

Christmas with you?" Rusty asked. "You have plenty going on in your life right now."

She deserved an answer but Trent wasn't entirely certain what response to give her.

The trouble was that he'd been expecting a completely different sort of woman to respond to the profile—one who wouldn't have questioned him. One who'd quietly throw in the towel and go home when he indicated no interest in her. Not one who challenged him and provoked him into kissing her.

"I'd hoped to be finished with the contracts by now." True. "And my uncles were looking forward to your visit. They were thrilled when you asked to bring your grandmother. I didn't want to disappoint them just because my timing was off."

He wondered if he should apologize. Rusty held herself very still, looking at him with an expression he couldn't read.

Then her brown eyes softened and the side of her mouth pulled upward. "You're a decent guy, Trent. And I understand—better than you might expect. You see—"

Rusty's comment was interrupted by a tapping on the open door. Agnes walked in. "These came for you, Trent." She handed him three overnight delivery envelopes.

"Thanks." More files from his office. He tossed the cardboard envelopes onto the floor beside all the other papers he needed to review later.

"Doc thought you might be back here working." Agnes leveled a stern look at the computer. "It's a lovely afternoon and you two shouldn't be cooped up here in the *bedroom*." She raised her eyebrows at Rusty, who promptly rolled her eyes. "Rusty, we used those Georgia pecans from the pantry in our cookies."

"Is that bad?"

"No, but Harvey claims he can tell the difference between those nuts and the ones they pick here at the ranch. He insists that Triple D pecans would be best for our Christmas cooking. We need more. Now, if you two will gather pecans, I'll make a pecan pie for tonight. What do you say?"

Taking a break suddenly appealed to Trent. "I like pecan pie."

"Have you ever had pecan ice cream sauce?" asked Rusty with a look at her grandmother.

"No, can't say that I have."

She laughed. "You just might get the chance."

The weather was cool enough to wear jackets, but not really cold. Armed with sacks, Trent and Rusty walked toward the pecan trees behind the ranch house.

"The time to pick pecans was in November," Trent said. "Harvey knows that. I'm surprised he didn't pick this year."

"News flash," Rusty said. "They were trying to get us out of your bedroom."

Oh. "We're not a couple of teenagers. Nothing improper is going to happen in there," Trent protested.

"Too bad. You're a great kisser." Tossing an impish grin over her shoulder, Rusty started jogging.

She liked the way he kissed. Trent grinned, ignoring all his internal alarms. He was supposed to be alienating her. The trouble was, he hadn't expected to *like* any woman his uncles found with that ad. Never would he have picked Rusty for the type of woman to respond to it.

But something about the profile had appealed to her or she wouldn't be here. Therefore, she not only assumed he was the man described, she wanted that sort of man.

And he was not that sort of man.

What a mess. He should turn around now and head back to his bedroom. Alone.

"Come on, Creighton, get the lead out!" Laughter peppered Rusty's voice.

Trent wasn't a jogger. Running after her and not catching her would be humiliating. Catching her might be worse. He started jogging.

He was going to regret this.

Trent gave a halfhearted chase, but Rusty was sidetracked by something she saw or heard near the big old barn on the way to the grove of trees.

"Does Doc keep his animals in here?" She wasn't even breathing hard.

Trent nearly passed out trying to pretend he wasn't breathing hard, either. "No." He pointed to the low, metal building and pen east of the barn. "That's where they are. He wanted a modern facility and added on to his old vet clinic four years ago."

"Then what's in here?"

Trent shrugged. "Not much. Harvey uses it for storage."

"I thought I heard something." She looked up at him in that way women have when they expect you to do something.

"You want me to check?"

"Don't *you* want to?"

"Not particularly. I want to find plenty of pecans for your grandmother to make a pie."

"Yeah, we'll have to get extra in case she ne—wants to make more than one," Rusty muttered. She tugged at the wooden bar holding the door closed.

Resigned, Trent helped her.

Creaking, the big double doors swung toward them a few feet. Trent pulled one side open and stared into the black interior.

"It's dark in there. Is there a light switch?" Rusty felt along the sides of the inner wall.

"It *is* dark." Trent couldn't shake the feeling that something was off. "Too dark. Usually light shines through the cracks and seams in the wooden siding."

Just then Rusty's hand connected with a switch. Scattered bare light bulbs valiantly attempted to relieve the gloom.

Stunned, Trent gazed around him. Boxes, cartons and crates were stacked floor to rafter, blocking out any daylight that would have normally seeped inside the barn.

"Look at all this junk!" Rusty wandered to the nearest brown column, which appeared to have been recently shoved inside. One of the boxes was upside down and must have fallen, causing the sound Rusty had heard.

"'L.L. Bean, Sharper Image, DAK...' This is a monument to mail order." She turned to face him. "Your uncles are power shoppers."

"This place is a warehouse." Tracing his fingers over the cartons, Trent walked to the end of the row. What he found there brought a reluctant chuckle.

"What?" Rusty joined him.

Trent pointed to three beds. "Harvey's mattress-testing facility."

Rusty bounced on one. "This bed's too hard," she said in a little girl voice and moved to the next mattress. "This bed's too soft." Moving to the third, she sighed and stretched out on it. "And this bed's just right." Scooting over, she patted the space beside her. "Care to try it out for yourself?"

"I'll take your word for it." Seeing a warehouseful of unopened packages alarmed Trent. Normal people didn't stockpile massive quantities of . . . stuff like this.

"You were more fun to tease back in your bedroom." Rusty sat up and stuck out her lower lip.

"Sorry. I'm just surprised to see all this." Trent squeezed around the column of boxes to the bigger crates in back.

Rusty dropped the Goldilocks routine. "Didn't you know about it?"

"No." Farming equipment. New farming equipment. But the Davis brothers hadn't grown anything more than a vegetable garden in years.

The boxes around him shook as Rusty went exploring on her own.

"Careful," he called.

"Yeah. I'd be a little concerned about one of these towers falling on Harvey."

"Oh, I'm concerned all right."

"Trent."

The tone of her voice drew him. He found her standing next to a waist-level crate. "What did you find?"

"Medical equipment." She pointed. "Unless this is mislabeled, that's an ultrasound machine."

And a stand for it, too. Trent was speechless.

Rusty nudged him with her elbow. "When was the last time you checked their credit card limit?"

Trent leaned against the crate and rubbed his temple. "Because of their *excellent* credit rating, they don't have a limit."

"If they keep charging at this rate, they won't have that nasty excellent rating problem for much longer."

In spite of himself, Trent burst out laughing, then shook his head. "I don't know why I put up with my uncles."

"Because you love them," Rusty answered simply. "I know men don't like to say that word, but I can tell you love them by the way you act and watch out for them." There was a short silence before she continued grudgingly, "Don't get conceited, but it's one of your more appealing qualities."

"Thanks," he managed to choke out as emotions bombarded him. Not one woman he'd brought to the Triple D had ever understood how important his uncles were to him. Not one woman would have truly cared.

"They raised me," he told her. "My mother was their only sister."

"What happened?" Rusty circled back to Harvey's mattresses.

Trent followed her. "When I was seven, my parents were killed in a tour bus accident. I was visiting the

Triple D at the time and I just stayed on. Emma, Clarence's wife, was alive then and they took me in."

"You didn't have cousins?"

"No."

Rusty nodded as though mentally fitting a piece to a puzzle. "So Clarence must think of you as his son."

"Probably. He put me right to work, which kept me from moping around. That was back when the ranch was operating and before they struck it rich. I was a teenager when the well came in and nobody knew how to handle that amount of money."

Rusty started to laugh. "And now they do?"

Trent joined her. "No, but now they've got me to handle it for them."

"And a fine job you're doing, too."

"Hey, I'll have you know that I just turned down a request for a raise in their allowance."

"You're such a Scrooge," she said dryly.

As their laughter died away, he asked, "So, how about you? When did you lose your parents?"

"I never had any to lose," she answered promptly, and, as far as Trent could tell, without any bitterness. "You see, I understand how you feel about your uncles because I feel the same way about my grandmother. She raised me, so she's the one I consider to be my mother. My biological mother is Dr. Ellen Romero. The botanist?"

"Sorry, I haven't heard of her."

Rusty lifted a shoulder, then tugged the sweater back into place. "You'd have to be interested in that field. Her lifelong work has been to develop strains of agricultural plants that will thrive in arid conditions. She lives in Africa somewhere."

Rusty tossed out the last bit of information a bit too casually. She did care, no matter how much she tried to pretend otherwise.

"As I understand the story, she and my father, whom I've never met, were grad students living together. They applied for research grants and were told it would look better if they were married. So they got married and it worked. In fact, they were offered two grants. My father wanted one and my mother wanted the other. No problem—they divorced. Then Ellen discovered she was pregnant. Babies weren't allowed in whatever remote area she was going to be living in, so she decided to give me up for adoption. Gran insisted on raising me."

Trent was appalled by Rusty's parents. "Your grandmother sounds like a very special person."

"She is."

By the way she said it, Trent knew Rusty was just as protective of her grandmother as he was of his uncles.

"Gran was a single mother back when there weren't many single mothers and then she had to turn around and do it all over again with me. I know she thought Ellen would come back for me after a couple of years and be grateful, but Ellen's maternal feelings are directed toward her plants."

She was trying to be so tough, yet she was showing him a vulnerability that he found disturbingly appealing. "Do you ever see your mother?"

"Rarely. And I don't think of her as my 'mother.' I know it sounds strange, but she's more like an older sister or a distant cousin or something."

"So it's been just you and your grandmother?"

Rusty nodded.

Trent thought he now understood why Rusty had answered that profile his uncles had written. She'd never had a traditional family, so naturally, she was seeking one.

After what she'd just told him, he felt like scum. He should never have agreed to go along with his uncles' scheme.

6

AFTER THEY LEFT the warehouse, Rusty pretty much forgot about the pecans until she and Trent walked into the kitchen and encountered Agnes's expectant gaze. His mind obviously elsewhere, Trent hung his jacket on the coatrack by the door and stalked toward the den. Rusty thrust her empty sack behind her back and edged toward the pantry. Maybe she could steal some of those Georgia pecans from the cellophane wrapping. She doubted anyone would notice the difference.

"That was quick," commented Agnes with a speculative arch to her eyebrow.

"Mmm." Rusty quickly disappeared behind the pantry door.

"You two aren't squabbling, are you?"

Squabbling? Rusty made faces from inside the pantry. "I don't know Trent well enough to squabble with him," she said. Squabbling implied a relationship of some duration. Her grandmother was still living the home-and-hearth fantasy. Just goes to show what fresh, country air will do to a person.

"Well, good. Men don't like it at all."

"That's because they've usually done something wrong."

Rusty heard a sigh.

Searching the pantry, she discovered brown grocery bags filled with unshelled pecans. By the lack of the usual commercial packaging, she surmised that Harvey, indeed, had gone pecan picking. Her recent excursion with Trent had been a clumsy matchmaking ploy, which she should have anticipated. She needed to have a little talk with her grandmother. No matchmaking.

After all, she thought smugly, within hours of their arrival, Trent had kissed her. Okay, so it didn't mean anything, but technically, he *had* kissed her.

And technically, the kiss was great. There could be some serious perks to being a domestic slave.

Rusty was on her way to solicit nutcracking help from the uncles when she saw that Trent had reached them first. From their expressions, Rusty guessed that he was having a financial chat with them. Harvey looked stubborn, Clarence, indulgent, and Doc, bored. They hadn't lowered the footrests on their recliners, but Trent had taken control of the television remote and held it in crossed arms.

And no one was currently using the telephone.

What a glorious opportunity. Still carrying a sack of pecans, Rusty hurried to her room, grabbed her computer and within moments was sitting in Trent's desk chair reading alarming E-mail from Alisa.

"We need to talk," Alisa had written. No kidding.

Rusty pushed the unshelled pecans and Trent's shopaholic uncles out of her mind.

That rotten George Kaylee had commissioned photo illustrations of his proposal for the Next to Nature campaign. According to Alisa, they were top-notch professional.

George must feel the bonus he'd earn if he were successful was worth the personal financial investment. He'd also seen Rusty's trip out of town as the perfect opportunity to punch up his proposal without giving her time to counter with a little punching of her own.

This was serious. Rusty sat back and stared at her computer screen. She was using sketches that would be mounted on storyboards. By comparison, her campaign proposal wouldn't look as impressive, even if her ideas were better. Clients were funny that way. She's seen entire campaigns decided on something as trivial as the background color used for the presentation folders.

Checking her watch, Rusty decided to try to call Alisa even though it was after work hours in Chicago.

"Dearsing Agency. Rusty Romero's office."

"Alisa? You're still there on a Friday night? What a pro."

"Rusty! I've been about to go out of my mind! Why haven't you called?"

Rusty briefly explained the telephone situation at the Triple D. "I'm lucky I caught you."

"Lucky, nothing! I want you to get this account because then you'll be promoted. And if you're promoted, then *I'll* be promoted. But right now, it doesn't look good for the home team."

The phone line clicked and Rusty heard Harvey call, "What's that order number?" before piercing tones blasted her ear.

"Excuse me? Mr. Davis?"

"I'd like two dozen wire deer, dear."

"No, it's Rusty."

"At that price they shouldn't rust. Isn't the wire coated with white vinyl?"

"Mr. Davis—it's Rusty Romero. I'm on the extension."

"Oh, Miss Rusty. Are you ordering the wire deer, too?"

"No, I'm speaking to a friend of mine."

"Is she taking orders for the deer?"

"No...yes. Yes, she is." Truly, it was easier this way. "Go ahead and give her your order." Now Rusty'd have to remember to order the stupid deer herself.

After Harvey ordered his herd of deer from a bemused Alisa and got off the telephone, Rusty sighed. "You see? Listen, do you suppose you could get a closer look at George's campaign? I don't want you to do anything to jeopardize your job, but—"

"I'm ahead of you. As we speak, I'm holding photographs in my hot little hand."

Rusty's heart picked up speed. Alisa was the best. "How did you get them?"

"Out of George's garbage. They're outtakes, but ought to give you the general idea."

"You're kidding." What a break. "Why didn't he shred them?"

"He told Tammy to, but she had a date, so I offered to shred the garbage for her."

"Aren't you a pal." Rusty gave a low whistle. "She won't make that mistake again."

"I know." Alisa sighed. "You can only use the garbage bit with newbies once before they catch on. Shall

I send the pictures to you, or are you coming back soon?"

Rusty closed her eyes. Originally she'd assumed her grandmother would quickly tire of cooking for strangers and want to leave well before Christmas. Unfortunately it appeared that just the opposite had happened. Agnes was in homemaker heaven and was reveling in the uncles' company. Rusty couldn't remember the last time she'd seen her grandmother so animated.

Dragging her back to Chicago now would be cruel. And had Agnes ever asked her for anything before? It was time for Rusty to be unselfish.

"Better overnight the pictures," she said to Alisa.

"Okay, except the mail's gone out for the day and there's no overnight delivery in the hinterlands. It'll be Monday before you get them."

"Nuts. Hey, can you fax me copies tonight, so I can get a general idea of what he's doing?" There was no way Rusty could wait until Monday to see George's pictures. Even though the copies would be awful, it was better than nothing.

"Fax now?"

"Uh..." Harvey would undoubtedly interrupt the transmission. This single telephone line was the pits. "It'll have to be later tonight."

"What time?"

Good question. After everyone had gone to bed would be best, but that would be imposing on Trent. What choice did she have? "Midnight?"

"I'll put the fax on automatic," Alisa responded.

"Oh, and, Alisa? Since you've got all the information, will you please order the deer?"

AS SHE WORKED on her laptop that night, Rusty vowed to find a way to install another phone line. Why Trent hadn't done so before now was beyond her. Unless he thought that by keeping the uncles limited to one telephone line he'd cut back on their ordering.

Like that had really worked. She thought of the barn and shook her head. She didn't envy Trent *that* problem. Besides, she had her own difficulties. Agnes had been annoyed that Rusty hadn't joined her in the kitchen—not because of the extra work, but because there wasn't any way Rusty could take credit for cooking dinner.

In spite of her grandmother's promise not to make it again, dinner had been tuna noodle casserole, and frankly, Rusty had been happy to give full credit to Agnes for that dish. Still, Agnes was concerned that Rusty wasn't acting the part of Supreme Domestic Goddess. Rusty wasn't worried. Trent had been so preoccupied, he hadn't even noticed her culinary talents. Or lack of.

Rusty shifted in the bed so she could see the clock. It was eleven forty-five. Pulling on her robe, she closed her laptop and slid her stocking feet carefully across the wooden floor, hoping to avoid telltale creaking. Pulling open her door, she peered into the hallway.

Unless Trent had fallen asleep with the light on in his room, he was still awake. One problem averted.

Unfortunately, his light wasn't the only one on. Either Clarence or Doc must be the night owl, since Harvey was still testing mattresses in the barn.

She crept toward Trent's room, conscious of the irony in the situation. Here she was, sneaking into an attractive bachelor's room in the middle of the night to receive a fax. Perhaps her priorities *could* stand an overhaul.

Reaching Trent's closed door, Rusty hesitated before tapping. Sounds carried at night and she didn't want to be discovered by whichever uncle was still awake.

She tapped lightly and winced. No response. Leaning her ear against the door, she heard shuffling and pulled back just as Trent opened the door.

"Hi, can I—" It was at that point that Rusty noticed Trent wasn't wearing a shirt.

All the air left her lungs.

Gray sweatpants rode low on his hips, his feet were encased in thick white socks and he was wearing black wire-rimmed glasses.

He looked great. He looked more than great—he looked casual manly great. And since he hadn't been expecting company, this was his natural manly state. And his natural manly state was . . . great. Really, really great.

His natural manly state was affecting her vocabulary. There were no words left in her oxygen-starved brain.

"Can you what?"

He'd spoken. Rusty knew she should respond but she seemed incapable of it. Besides, she'd forgotten why she'd come to his room anyway. The original reason didn't matter. There was the issue of a shirtless Trent to be dealt with. Delightful possibilities arrayed themselves before her, all of them involving ways to come in contact with Trent and his chest. Any other incidental body contact would be welcome, too.

Where had he been hiding those muscles? Rusty's mental image of the perfect male physique rapidly morphed into Trent.

He had strong shoulders and subtly defined pectorals, with just enough chest hair to enhance rather than detract. Rusty wasn't a hairy chest aficionado, and while Trent's chest wasn't exactly *hairy,* neither was it entirely smooth. Just right, as a matter of fact. Why hadn't she realized how utterly *male* chest hair was before?

Especially the dark patch in the center. Rusty's gaze fastened upon it as she mentally buried her fingers in the curls.

"Rusty?" Trent spoke to the top of her head, since Rusty was staring at his chest.

"Mmm?"

"It's the middle of the night and you're standing in my doorway."

"Yes." She let her eyes travel upward. It was his neck. That was it. He had a lovely long neck that disguised his scrumptious muscles. In fact, his neck was almost as good as his chest. What an unexpected delight. Necks as an erogenous zone. Who'd have thought it?

"Are you coming in?" He stepped aside.

"Yes, please." She took a few steps forward, then stopped. There was an interesting hollow at the side of his neck where the shoulder sloped up to meet it. A little indentation just waiting to be filled with kisses. Rusty would have sighed if she'd had any air in her lungs to sigh with.

Trent raised his eyebrows.

She should say something. "You have a neck." Hmm. Perhaps she should have said something else.

He drew his hands to his waist, the movement deepening the indentation that so fascinated her. "Most people do."

"Well . . . some men don't have much of a neck. You do, though. It's . . . nice. A nice neck." *Shut up!*

"Thank you," he said gravely.

In the silence that followed, the corner of his mouth quivered. "You brought your computer." He pointed to the forgotten weight in her arms. "Therefore, I'm assuming this is *not* a midnight seduction attempt."

"It didn't start out that way," Rusty murmured.

"And now?"

She sighed regretfully. "Probably not."

"In that case, I should put on my shirt." He reached for the garment hanging on the closet doorknob.

Cover up his chest? "Don't go to any trouble on my account."

He paused in the act of shrugging into his shirt, blinked twice and grinned the smug grin a man gets when he knows a woman is attracted to him. "You're sure this isn't a seduction?"

Teeth. Dimples. The chest and neck she'd so admired. "No . . ."

His grin widened. "How about I just leave the shirt unbuttoned while you decide?"

"Okay." Rusty took a deep breath, followed by another to jump-start her brain.

Her brain remembered the fax. "My fax! What time is it?"

"Almost midnight."

Yelping, Rusty dived for the phone jack. "Can I hook up my modem?" She jerked out Trent's modem line. Oops. His computer wasn't on, was it?

"Go ahead." Trent sat on the bed.

Rusty couldn't believe she'd been sidetracked by Trent's chest. Okay, his neck, too, but necks, she saw all the time. She shouldn't have been sidetracked by a mere neck. And she was an intelligent, ambitious woman who was not normally overcome by the sight of a bare male chest, either.

Which meant that there was something about *this* male chest that was different.

The fact that it belonged to Trent?

From under the desk, Rusty peered at him. Bespectacled, he sat on the bed and stared at a paper. Then he put it down and picked up another one, rubbed his forehead and picked up the first again.

No, she decided from her crouched position, it wasn't Trent. It couldn't be Trent. He happened to be in the vicinity, that's all. It must be the effect fresh, country air had on her. That fresh air was lethal. It turned her grandmother into a domestic zombie and attacked Rusty's hormones.

She should cut down on breathing. But look what had happened when she'd tried that moments ago. No, maybe she should go find some pollution to breathe and counteract all that fresh air.

Backing out from under the desk, Rusty stood and brushed at her knees. She was wearing the robe her grandmother hated. Agnes had a point that Rusty only now fully appreciated. Nope. She sighed a regretful sigh. No seduction possible at this time. "I'm receiving several pages, so it'll be a few minutes. Should I come back later or . . ."

Without looking up from the papers, Trent waved vaguely. "Have a seat."

Gingerly, Rusty moved a small paper pile and sat on the trunk.

Exactly at midnight, the telephone rang and her modem picked it up. Rusty bounded over to watch until she saw that the connection had been made. Now all she had to do was wait.

"You don't think the phone woke up anyone, do you?"

Trent shook his head. Tossing a file folder onto the bed, he removed his glasses and rubbed the bridge of his nose. He looked tired.

"I didn't know you wore glasses," Rusty said. Wasn't she the witty conversationalist.

"I took out my contacts."

Of course he had. Any normal person would have been able to figure that out. It was just that she couldn't stop staring at him and figured she'd better say something to have an excuse to keep looking at him.

"What did your uncles have to say about all the stuff in the barn?"

Trent gave her a doleful look. "Christmas presents."

Rusty's eyes widened. "Whoa."

"They were very cagey. Tried the old don't-ask-too-many-questions-around-Christmas routine. But since I haven't asked for any farm equipment under my tree, I mentioned the unusual quantity and *variety* of items in the barn."

"And?"

He sighed. "They told me to mind my own business. I pointed out that their financial well-being *was* my business and once we established that they could afford this little shopping spree, they wrestled me for the TV remote and sent me out of the room."

Rusty burst into laughter. The thought of those three couch potatoes wrestling their muscular nephew was too much.

"I'm glad you're amused."

Trying to stifle her laughter, Rusty asked, "They really *can* afford all that?"

Trent nodded.

"Wow." Then they ought to be able to afford a second—or even third telephone line. She wondered how to broach the subject.

"Rusty?"

"Yes?"

She could see him choose his words.

"As an outsider, you...uh, you haven't noticed anything mentally off-kilter with them, have you?"

Rusty sobered immediately. She could tell Trent was seriously concerned. "No," she answered with equal seriousness. "Now, Harvey is a little unusual..."

"That's just Harvey."

"I thought so. And my grandmother would have said something to me if she thought anything was wrong. She worked in real estate before she retired and learned to size up people quickly."

"Good." Trent closed his eyes in relief. "I'll have to assume my uncles have their reasons for stockpiling all that stuff."

His obvious concern for his uncles added points in the "good guy" column. Trent was racking up a lot of positive points lately, Rusty noted. Almost enough to counter the negative ones he'd started with.

How had that happened? Dragging her eyes away from him, Rusty searched for another topic of conversation.

"Are those your bids?" She indicated the folders spread over the bedspread.

"Yes." Changing the subject seemed to suit him. "I hope more will come in, but I thought I'd start comparing and eliminating now."

"Hey." Rusty recognized a familiar logo. "I know this company." Without considering that she might be looking at material Trent would rather not share with her, Rusty picked up a folder that had been set away from the others.

"Lance Construction." She shook her head. "I can't believe they're still in business."

"You know that company?" He spoke sharply.

Nodding, Rusty decided it didn't really matter if she told Trent about her work. He probably wondered why she was receiving faxes in the middle of the night, anyway. "I work for the Dearsing Ad Agency in Chicago." She hooked a thumb over her shoulder. "That's what the faxes are about."

Trent lifted his hand, palm outward. "You don't have to explain."

No, but I thought you'd at least be curious. His disinterest was probably just as well. "Anyway, back when I was very green, Lance Construction offered Dearsing their account. The dollar figure they threw around meant a huge budget for the lucky account exec." Rusty shrugged. "Naturally, I thought I'd take a crack at it, along with everybody else. So they sat and looked at all the presentations, nodded their heads and offered a contract for a fraction of the original budget they'd mentioned. Dearsing couldn't do the campaign they'd selected for that amount. The deal was off and Lance Construction proceeded to use in-house staff—with our ideas."

"You had no recourse?"

Rusty grimaced. "Oh, they changed everything just enough to avoid a lawsuit. Believe me, I'm certain Dearsing explored the options." She picked up the folder and pointed to the logo. "See the knight on horseback with the lance? That was my idea. Not that I was ever going to get the credit, but still."

"Why wouldn't you get credit if your idea was used?"

Rusty looked up at him. "Because that wasn't my job. I was just a general project assistant—a glorified errand girl. I was in on the brainstorming and showed my sketch to one of the account executives."

"And he stole it?"

Rusty waved her hands. Trent was beginning to look outraged on her behalf and she hastened to set him straight. "No, I was thrilled he used it, because I wanted him to request me for a staff position if he got the project. That's how people work their way up at Dearsing."

Trent's forehead smoothed. "So you have to pay your dues first."

"Right. But I got off track about Lance Construction. Bait and switch is their modus operandi. They lowball a bid—they did, didn't they?"

Slowly, Trent nodded.

"They get the job and midway through, they need more money. In fact, there was some government building in Chicago they were supposed to build and the situation was so bad, it was in the papers for weeks. Taxpayer money and all that. I guess that's where you heard about them." Rusty handed him the folder. "They've got a *major* PR problem."

Trent looked at the folder, then back at her. "I—you're sure this is the same company?"

"Based in a little town in Illinois?"

"Yes."

Standing, Rusty spread her hands. "How many other firms like that can there be?" She stepped over to the computer and saw that it was still receiving. Alisa must have recovered a ton of pictures. Returning to the trunk at the foot of the bed, Rusty saw that Trent was staring at the Lance Construction folder.

It was a great-looking folder, if she did say so herself. Along with her knight idea, they'd appropriated the black and silver-blue color scheme that had been George Kaylee's idea. Probably his last good one, she thought disparagingly. He'd been an account executive then and she'd been eager to have him select her for a project. George was very good at selecting and using the best ideas.

Unfortunately, he wasn't good at generating them and after several months, Rusty chafed at the lack of recognition.

Those were the days. She sighed and wondered whose ideas he'd used for his Next to Nature campaign.

"Rusty?"

Trent recaptured her attention. He'd put his glasses back on. Honestly, the man looked like a commercial for loungewear. That chest of his was something.

"I had *not* heard anything adverse about Lance Construction and I was seriously considering going with them."

It took a moment for Trent's words to register. "I assumed if *I* knew about them, everybody in the construction industry knew about them." She concentrated on trying to remember when the big flap over the public building had occurred. "Check the Chicago papers about four or five years ago. I can't remember exactly when it was, but I do remember gloating over their troubles." She grinned.

"I'll have my assistant check it out." He pressed his lips together. "As she should have done before forwarding this bid to me." He chucked the folder against the wall. It slid down and disappeared behind the bed.

"Thanks for the heads-up," he said. "You saved me considerable time."

Rusty waved off his compliment, though it pleased her. "You wouldn't have contracted with them without investigating."

"No, but I might not have had time to investigate anyone else after I found out they weren't suitable. I owe you."

An incredibly good-looking man with a great chest and lovely neck was indebted to her. Life didn't get much better than this.

As Trent gathered up the various papers and files spread over the bed, Rusty spent several pleasurable moments fantasizing about ways he might repay his debt.

He stacked the folders on the floor beside the bed and leaned against the headboard, lacing his fingers over his stomach.

This pose drew attention to his chest, which was already prominently featured in Rusty's repayment fantasies.

"You know, you're not anything like I expected." His eyes drifted over her, making Rusty acutely conscious of her unmade-up face and ratty robe.

She should have listened to her grandmother, but she'd never expected to find herself wearing the robe in front of Trent, or the Trent who'd placed that "traditional wife" profile.

"What were you expecting?" she asked cautiously.

"Someone more—" he gestured "—aggressively domestic."

"What, like hitting you on the head with a rolling pin? I considered it a time or two."

Laughing, Trent took off his glasses and set them on the bedside table. Rearranging the pillows, he said, "Yes, we've both avoided mentioning that time I was out of line. I apologize."

She'd been referring to his views on women's roles. "Please don't. Then I'll have to apologize for that crack I made and . . . I don't want to."

Trent blinked.

Rusty smiled benignly.

Trent cleared his throat. "Clarence really chewed me out about not spending more time with you." His expression warmed. "I'm beginning to think he had a good point."

Uh-oh. Just when she needed to spend more time at the computer herself. "It's okay. I know you've got this deal in the works and you're busy."

"Even so—"

"No, really. Take as much time as you need."

His eyes narrowed thoughtfully. "You're very understanding for someone who traveled all this way to spend her Christmas holiday with strangers."

"That's the way the cookie crumbles." She laughed weakly. All these food references—she'd better quit it before he really thought about how much "help" her grandmother had given her in the kitchen. Taken over for her, was more the case.

Her computer beeped, signaling the end of Alisa's transmission. Rusty jumped up. "Well, looks like I'm finished here," she announced brightly, and scuttled over to disconnect her computer.

"Tell me something," Trent said as she ducked beneath the desk. "You're obviously intelligent and you have a job that requires you to stay in contact with your office. Why do you want to give that all up and move to the country?"

His question caught her so off guard that Rusty froze in her crouched position. What on earth could she say?

Rusty wished she could just confess that she wasn't interested in the position of "traditional wife" as advertised but was willing to negotiate anything else Trent had in mind. He'd probably be shocked and kick her out. Wouldn't her grandmother be pleased if Rusty was asked to leave over matters of moral turpitude?

She emerged from under the desk, to find Trent standing there, just inches away, regarding her closely.

Rusty smiled, perhaps a bit too widely. "I think change can be good for people." *Like you changing your views about women.* From what he'd told her, his poor aunt Emma had cooked and cleaned for everybody. No wonder he expected the same from Rusty.

"And you think this is a good change?"

Hardly. "Well, there was just something about your profile." *An irritating something.* "I don't meet too many men who are so up front about marriage and children."

Trent studied her. "You liked that part?"

Are you kidding? "You'd obviously put a lot of thought into your future and laid it right out there." Rusty slid her arm sideways. "No woman could possibly misunderstand what you want in a wife."

Trent said nothing.

She probably hadn't sounded very positive. "Actually, I do find it refreshing to know a man's views on marriage and family before I become involved with him." *Especially if I don't agree with them.* "It . . . saves time." Rusty let her words trail off, wondering if she should keep talking or quit now.

She could see Trent mulling over what she'd said, which she hoped sounded like a fair explanation.

Involved with him. Inwardly sighing, Rusty wished she hadn't spoken that last part out loud, especially with Trent's chest inches in front of her.

After her little speech, any physical overtures on her part would certainly indicate her acceptance of Trent's archaic views of family life. What rotten luck. Unless . . .

Unless Trent made the first physical overture. That might work. Just when things were heating up, she could drop little hints about having second thoughts concerning the whole kids-in-the-country bit. He'd murmur away her objections, as men are known to do when in the throes of passion, and things could proceed nicely. Then later, it wouldn't be a complete surprise when Rusty told him being a ranch wife wasn't for her.

Sounded like a plan.

Now, for the plan to work, she would have to subtly encourage him. Perhaps she'd arrange for some additional midnight faxes and arrive to receive them dressed in more alluring attire.

"Yes, it does help to know exactly what a person expects from a relationship," Trent was saying. "That way, no one's disappointed."

She watched as his gaze traveled over her face, coming to rest on her lips. Rusty was reminded of the kiss they'd shared, and shivered.

"You're cold. I should let you get back to your room." With a hand at the small of her back, he guided her to the door.

Rusty scoured her mind for an excuse to stay.

"Oh, and don't worry about a repeat of my earlier behavior." He rubbed his temple and smiled disarmingly. "I promise it won't happen again."

No! "I'm not worried, in fact—"

"It's okay, Rusty. Chalk it up to an uncharacteristic impulse." Smiling platonically, he stuck out his hand. "Good night."

That chest. That neck. Those lips. With a silent whimper of regret, Rusty shook his hand good-night.

7

WHEN THE ALARM went off the next morning, Rusty had
slept only a few hours. Between unwelcome thoughts
of Trent and trying to decipher the details in the faxed
pictures, she didn't get to sleep until nearly three
o'clock.

It was now five-thirty, as her alarm persisted in re-
minding her. Rusty batted at it and groaned. This
morning she was determined to get up and fix breakfast all by herself. Last night it had seemed vitally important that she do so, if only to prove that she could,
but in the predawn darkness, she was much less enthusiastic.

Rusty reached for her robe, reconsidered, dropped
it back onto the chair and got dressed. There was no
way her eyes would tolerate makeup just now, so she
avoided looking in the mirror as she stumbled past it
on the way into the cold kitchen.

A light was already on and when she looked out the
back door she could see lights burning in Doc's animal
shed. He was up and she guessed he'd been up early
yesterday, too, and had caught her grandmother cooking. Well, this morning he'd catch Rusty cooking.

Now, what to cook? she wondered, rubbing her
arms.

Biscuits seemed to be a big hit and she'd just about gotten the hang of pancakes. That was two breads. Perhaps something from another food group.

Pulling open the refrigerator, Rusty took out buttermilk and the ham. Then she put back the ham. She was tired of ham. Besides, if she ingested any more salt, she'd stay bloated until Christmas.

Bacon. Another fatty, salty meat. Oh, well. She didn't have to eat it. Eggs seemed to be expected, so she pulled out those, as well. Brightening, she remembered Harvey's fruit and checked the ripening bowl. Two more pears. She decided to eat one all by herself right now.

Humming, Rusty bit into the pear and went to make coffee. While it brewed, she studied the cookbooks her grandmother had brought with her. The kitchen boasted several others, but Rusty didn't feel experienced enough to stray from anything with which she was acquainted, no matter how superficially.

Okay, where was the biscuit recipe? Rusty flipped through the bread section. There, biscuits. And more biscuits. She turned the page. Yet more biscuits. Drop biscuits, whole wheat, rolled, buttermilk, yeast, soda and cheese. Rich biscuits, egg biscuits, sour cream biscuits, corn meal . . . Rusty panicked. Other than popping open a can, how was she to have known that there was more than one way to make biscuits?

Which recipe had her grandmother made? Which one should she tackle? Rusty was not about to make such a momentous decision without coffee. As soon as she could pour a cup from the still-brewing pot, she did so and took a swallow.

That was better. While the caffeine kicked in, Rusty looked up pancakes. Buttermilk, whole wheat...good grief. She knocked back the entire cup of coffee before a replacement cup had dripped into the pot.

She would make her selection logically and choose the recipe with the least ingredients.

Fortified with another cup of coffee, Rusty began assembling the ingredients for buttermilk biscuits. This wasn't so hard, she thought, stirring the dough and feeling competently domestic for the first time in her life.

The feeling didn't last. She dumped the dough onto the butcher block and *then* read that she should have floured the surface first. Fine. Scraping runaway dough back into the bowl, Rusty cleaned off the counter, in the process discovering the tenacious sticking properties of wet flour, dried the countertop, spread flour over it and plopped the dough on top.

A white cloud poofed out and settled all over her black jeans. She, of course, was not wearing the infamous cow apron, but now wished she was.

Never mind. Rusty grabbed a rolling pin and started rolling. All she managed to accomplish was to coat the pin with sticky dough.

She cleaned it off and tried again with the same results. The dough was too sticky. Rusty added more flour and mixed everything with her hands until she had a nice stiff lump. Perhaps a bit *too* stiff, but by pounding instead of rolling, she was finally able to flatten the dough enough to cut out several circles of varying thicknesses.

Nearly an hour had passed since she'd entered the kitchen and this was all she'd accomplished. But it was a start, she told herself as she pushed the biscuits into the oven.

Rusty decided to tackle bacon and eggs next. Maybe she'd skip pancakes this morning.

Leaving the mess on the butcher block for later, Rusty grabbed for the iron skillets she'd washed yesterday. Slamming them on the stove, she lit the burners and ripped open the package of bacon, then stared.

The skillets were coated in rust. What had happened? She couldn't cook in rusty skillets. She might not be experienced, but she knew that much.

Dawn pinked the sky by the time Rusty had scoured the skillets and returned to the stove. She dumped the entire package of bacon into the skillet and went to set the table.

She returned to a smoking mass, grabbed the handle of the skillet and burned herself. Retrieving the stupid cow oven mitts, she raced to the back door and held the smoking pan outside. Wouldn't it be charming to awaken the household with the smoke alarm? Rusty held the door wider, hoping for a draft to dissipate the smoke. When she thought it was safe, she brought the pan back inside.

Okay, too much heat on the bacon. Next time she'd know. But that didn't save the bacon this time. Rusty tried in vain to separate the strips, but they were burned to the bottom of the pan. She salvaged the parts not directly in contact with the skillet, but it made for some strange-looking strips of bacon.

Eggs. She'd simply arrange a mound of fluffy, yellow scrambled eggs over the bacon and maybe no one would notice.

Rusty cracked a whole dozen eggs into a bowl, beat as much air into them as she could and poured them into a fresh skillet over more moderate heat.

While she watched the eggs, she arranged pieces of bacon on a platter. This could work. It wasn't so bad.

She could still smell the burned bacon, which meant everyone else would smell it, too. Rusty propped open the kitchen door and searched for an aerosol room freshener under the sink. When she didn't find one, she considered running back to her room for her perfume and shooting a few squirts of that around.

But first, the eggs. Rusty stirred them and discovered that in spite of the low flame, they were sticking to the pan. She stirred harder and dislodged bits of egg and ominous black particles, which reminded her that she hadn't added pepper. She did so now, hoping for the best.

As the eggs scrambled, they turned from the yellow she'd expected to a black-flecked gray. And they were still sticking to the pan.

What was the matter? She pulled the eggs off the heat. Until she figured out what had gone wrong, it didn't make sense to waste more.

The scorched smell was as strong as ever. Rusty fanned her oven mitts at the stove. Well, at least she still had the biscuits. And coffee. And the bacon wasn't too bad. She tried a lump of the scrambled eggs. They tasted fine, except for the crunchy black things that appeared to be pieces of the cast-iron skillet. She wished the eggs had stayed yellow.

As she stared at the unappetizing mass, an idea formed. Food coloring. Well, why not? Everyone had eaten it in cookie icing yesterday and eggs were food. Or they had been until she'd messed with them.

Rusty trotted over to the cabinet where spices and baking supplies were stored, found the yellow food coloring and, with a guilty look around the kitchen and out to Doc's shed, she squirted a yellow stream onto the eggs. By smashing the eggs with a fork, she managed to incorporate enough yellow dye to offset the gray. The result, while not entirely natural-looking, was better than it had been. She'd keep the curtains drawn, the lights low and hope for the best.

Rusty decided to celebrate with more coffee. On the way to the pot, she opened the oven door to check on the biscuits.

A blast of heat was accompanied by an overwhelming scorched odor. Frantically, Rusty removed the pan and stared at a dozen misshapen dark brown lumps. She'd forgotten to set the timer.

Disgusted with herself, Rusty slammed the baking tray on top of the mess on the butcher block and re-filled her coffee cup. Leaning against the counter, she surveyed the disastrous results of her cooking attempts. Realistically, what could she salvage?

Not much.

She wouldn't panic; situations had appeared bleak before. After all, she shouldn't have expected culinary perfection on her first attempt.

But she *had* expected better than this. What was wrong with her? Cooking couldn't be that hard. People in every culture around the world had cooked since the discovery of fire. Some of that ability had to be encoded in the genes. Obviously a recessive gene in her case.

Walking over to the butcher block, she poked at the biscuits and pried one off the baking sheet. Rock hard. Her failure was complete.

Rusty hurled the biscuit out the kitchen door. All she'd had to do was cook a simple breakfast so she could get back to her real work. Important work. Not stupid, mindless cooking. Not spending hours in the stupid kitchen, stuck on a stupid ranch, miles away from a decent carryout restaurant, trying to impress some stupid man.

Sniffing back frustrated tears, Rusty grabbed a wad of paper napkins and buried her face in them. Crying was stupid. Everything was stupid.

George Kaylee was stupid.

No, George Kaylee was *not* stupid, unfortunately. George was no doubt thrilled that his closest competitor had inexplicably chosen to take these critical days off. He'd be dancing in the streets if he learned that her stay was supposed to stretch as long as two weeks.

Of course, there was no chance of that now. Rusty was just moments away from being unmasked as the domestic impostor that she was, at which point she and her grandmother would be sent back to Chicago in humiliating defeat.

Yesterday that would have thrilled her. Yet today, incomprehensibly and irrationally, Rusty didn't want to leave in defeat. She wanted to be the one who chose to leave—preferably after everyone had enjoyed a gourmet breakfast she'd prepared with her own two hands.

After a few minutes of blubbering self-pity, she felt better. She rarely cried, but when she felt like it, Rusty discovered it was best to give in and get it over with, then fix whatever problem had upset her in the first place. The problem now was the lack of food and lack of time to fix it. Sighing, she decided to start over anyway.

She'd just blown her nose when she realized she wasn't alone.

Jerking her head up, she caught Trent sneaking into the kitchen.

He looked guilty. "I smelled . . . uh, I could tell you were cooking and thought I might grab a cup of coffee?"

Rusty wadded the napkins and wished she'd thrown *all* the biscuits out the door.

Silently she watched Trent concentrate on the coffeepot and avoid her eyes.

A blue haze shrouded the kitchen, even though cold air flooded the room. Rusty said nothing. She did, however, stare at the food coloring on the stove in hopes she could levitate it into a cabinet before Trent discovered it.

He cleared his throat. "You, uh, need some help?"

"Does it *look* like I need help?"

Trent's gaze flicked around the room as he sipped his coffee. "Yes."

Rusty felt tears threaten again and closed her eyes. Never had she imagined becoming so overwrought about, of all things, a cooking failure. Obviously the lack of sleep and the stress of her work was playing a big part in her weepiness. Whatever, she wished Trent would say what he was going to say and be done with it.

She felt, rather than heard, him approach her.

"You know, you make a *great* cup of coffee," he said, leaning against the counter next to her.

Rusty gave a watery chuckle. "Apparently that is the *only* thing I can make."

"No, you . . ." He glanced behind them. "Okay, the biscuits are a little brown."

"They're burned." Which, judging by the density of the one she'd thrown out the door, was a good thing. "I forgot to set the oven timer."

"That can happen to anybody. Just make toast this morning. I see you've got . . . bacon?" Trent sounded doubtful.

"Stuck to the pan." She watched as he poked at the pink and charred bits on the platter.

"So it's extra crispy . . . in places." He held up one of the only whole strips. "Look, you even managed crispy and limp on the same strip in case anyone prefers both."

She sighed. "Give it up, Trent."

He tossed the bacon back onto the platter. "I'm going to have to, since I have *no* idea what's in the other pan."

"Scrambled eggs." Rusty moved to block his view of the food coloring.

"From what animal?"

"Very funny. They taste fine." She picked up the skillet. "I'm not trying to make excuses, but something is wrong with these skillets. This morning, they were coated with rust and all the food sticks."

"Sounds like you didn't reseason them."

"What?"

"These are made of cast iron." He hefted one. "They have to be seasoned with oil before you use them."

"You mean all the food has to be fried in oil?" She made a face.

"No, just after the pans have been scrubbed." He carefully set the skillet with the blackened bacon grease back onto the stove. "I figured you knew what you were doing when you attacked them with the steel wool yesterday."

The fact that she'd appeared competent enough to fool him yesterday momentarily mollified her. "Well, black gunk kept coming off and I figured they needed a good cleaning." Rusty remembered all the burned pancakes. Trent didn't mention them.

"You need to coat cast iron with some vegetable oil and bake it in the oven for a few hours to let the oil soak in. The oil keeps the iron from rusting and the food from sticking when you cook it."

How did he know all this? "You do that after every use? Give me stainless steel any day."

Trent laughed and shook his head. "No, only when you reseason the pans. In between times, don't scrub quite so hard when you're cleaning."

"Oh, ick." Rusty was no longer hungry.

Unfortunately, the others would be. "Well, I suppose I better mix up some more biscuits." She gazed unenthusiastically at the flour-encrusted butcher block and hoped everyone would want to skip breakfast to-day.

"'Morning." Wiping his feet on the mat outside the door, Doc nodded at them and stepped into the kitchen.

With a sinking feeling, Rusty watched the middle Davis brother's face as he took in the kitchen. Without changing expression, he paused at the stove, blinked at the eggs, glanced toward Trent, then Rusty, then back to Trent again.

"Stove can be cantankerous at times," he said, then nodded once more and kept walking.

TRENT REALLY FELT for Rusty, though he tried not to.

Her face whitened and she bit her lip as Doc walked into the other room. So she'd messed up a panful of biscuits. Big deal. Probably overseasoned the eggs, but that could be attributed to differences in taste. He wasn't going to attribute the bacon to anything.

But what was with Doc? The stove was never cantankerous. Harvey didn't allow cantankerous objects anywhere in the house. Besides, the stove was relatively new and the cast-iron skillets were from a line of cookware some chef had touted on television and were supposed to be of superior quality.

Or they had been until the Romero women had gotten hold of them. Trent doubted the skillets would ever be the same.

"Perhaps now that the oven is warmed up, the next batch of biscuits will turn out better." With a tight smile, Rusty collected the debris and carried it over to the sink. Jamming her foot on the metal flip-top trash can, she scraped the burned biscuits off the baking sheet. They clanged against the trash can like hail fall-ing on a tin roof.

As the metal lid crashed back into place, Rusty shot Trent a defiant glance and snatched up the cookbook.

"Hey, don't worry about making more. I'll just have cereal this morning." He started for the pantry.

"There are four other people besides you and me who have to eat." She slammed down the cookbook and began scrubbing the butcher block. "They'll be awake any minute."

Trent paused, his hand on a box of sugared cereal that he'd slipped past Harvey and hidden behind the oat-meal. He had work to do. He should just pour a bowl of cereal and carry it back to the bedroom. "There's plenty of cereal back here—"

"I am *not* going to feed your uncles cereal!"

"Why not?" Trent found two boxes of something re-sembling shredded tree bark.

"Because my grandmother and I are supposed to be cooking, not pouring!"

Trent hesitated, put back the cereal and heard him-self say, "Then let me help you."

"*You?*"

The astonished expression on her face was truly an-noying, but he'd offered to help and help he would. "Yes. May I have the cookbook?"

She surrendered it with a laugh. "This, I've got to see."

"Stick around and you might learn something." He could tell that jab really got to her.

Rusty started banging the skillets around as she washed the dishes. Trent was aware of her watching him and especially aware when she thunked the freshly washed rolling pin on the counter, barely missing his fingers.

"Sorry." Not looking sorry at all, she carried the skillets over to the stove.

"Come here." Trent hooked her arm and pulled her back to the counter. "The dough is ready to be rolled out."

She peered into the bowl. "So it is. Carry on."

"Not so fast." Trent handed her the rolling pin and went to wash his hands.

When he turned around, a pink-cheeked Rusty was glaring at a dough-covered rolling pin. "Why does it keep doing that?"

"Beats me." Drying his hands, Trent came to stand beside her. "The dough looks like it could use more flour."

"Then why didn't you put more in?"

"I followed the recipe."

"Well, so did I." Visibly exasperated, Rusty cleaned white glops off the rolling pin, dumped flour everywhere and attacked the biscuit dough.

Trent watched her frustrated struggles. "I thought baking was supposed to be soothing."

"Yeah, right." Rusty swiped at her bangs, leaving dough and flour smeared across her forehead.

Careful not to smile, Trent held out a towel, realized her hands were all doughy, and wiped her forehead off himself.

"Thanks," she said grudgingly.

"You're trying too hard at this. Here." Standing behind her, Trent placed his hands over hers on the rolling pin handles. She held herself stiffly. "Relax." Rusty dropped her shoulders. "Now, roll slowly." He demonstrated. "Back and forth."

Trent had intended to back off at this point—what did he know about rolling out dough?—but her hair was right under his nose and he could smell the shampoo she used, along with the smoke from her earlier cooking efforts. Her back pressed against his chest and he liked the way she fit against him when the movements of rolling out the dough brought her body in contact with his.

Back and forth. Back and forth.

Trent became aware of the suggestive rhythm and the fact that he was unconsciously echoing it. By now the dough was so thin they'd have the world's flattest biscuits, but he wasn't about to stop.

When Rusty's tongue crept to the corner of her mouth as she concentrated on the edges, Trent wanted to fling away the rolling pin and ravish her on the spot. Instead he dipped his head and grazed the back of her neck, hoping she'd think his touch was the unavoidable result of her reaching to the edges of the ever-widening circle.

"Is that enough?" She turned her head to look at him, bringing her mouth to within a millimeter of his.

"No. Not at all," he whispered.

Rusty's gaze fastened on his lips. She didn't move.

He remembered the feel of her mouth on his. But he'd promised her it would never happen again.

So help him, he was going to break that promise. Rusty's eyes fluttered shut as he moved toward her.

Footsteps sounded outside the kitchen. "Rusty, I can't believe I overslept. We've got—"

Skidding to a halt, Agnes stopped in the act of tying a belt around a satiny white robe and stared at them.

No one said anything, unless dual sighs from Rusty and Trent counted.

He straightened, careful to keep his movements slow, so Rusty's grandmother wouldn't think anything fishy was going on even though Trent knew there had been.

"Trent was helping me roll out the biscuit dough," Rusty said brightly.

Agnes finished tying her robe and grabbed the lapels, pulling them together over some lace thing she wore. She looked a lot different than she had yesterday morning, Trent thought.

"Trent...good morning." She patted at her hair and sent a wary look toward the stove.

"Good morning." Both women darted looks at each other and Trent decided to make his exit. "Let me know when the biscuits are done." He grabbed his coffee cup and headed out the door, regretfully glad Agnes had chosen that particular moment to enter the kitchen.

"WHAT'S GOING ON?" Agnes asked the minute Trent left. "It smells like you're burning the place down." She passed by the platter of bacon, picked up a piece and nodded. "Not bad, though."

"Oh, come on, Gran. It's awful."

"Bacon is inherently awful. The Davis brothers should be discouraged from eating it."

"I know *I'm* discouraged." Rusty turned to the biscuit dough.

"What is that?" Agnes pointed to the huge circle.

"My second batch of biscuits. Or, rather, Trent's batch."

"What happened to yours?"

Rusty pointed to the trash can.

"It's no wonder if you rolled the dough this thin. What were you trying to make, crackers?" Agnes folded the dough into quarters and mashed it together. "Try cutting them out now."

Rusty checked her watch and sighed. "Gran, why bother? Trent told me there's cereal in the pantry."

"Bite your tongue!" Agnes began to cut the biscuits herself. "We owe these men a hearty breakfast."

"Gran." Rusty stilled her hand. "The jig is up, as they say. I can't fake being able to cook any longer. Doc's already been by this morning. And you saw Trent—"

"Doc's been by already?" Agnes interrupted.

"Yes." Rusty eyed her grandmother's pinkening cheeks. "Is that why you're wearing your peignoir instead of your Homestead Hattie calico?"

"I—" Agnes looked down at herself. "That was an accident."

"Sure it was." Rusty grinned. Her grandmother and Doc? Stranger things had happened.

"Rachel Marie, have some respect for your grandmother. At least *I* didn't have some man 'helping' me roll out biscuits, of all things."

"It was *his* idea!" Rusty protested.

"*Was* it?" Agnes looked thoughtful.

Rusty didn't want her having those thoughts. "He was just being *nice*. Something I didn't think he was capable of." That wasn't really true. Rusty didn't know why she felt compelled to hide from her grandmother the fact that she found Trent not entirely repulsive. She only knew she did.

He'd helped her and hadn't said one word about her not being able to cook.

He wasn't such a bad guy, after all.

And he had a really great chest.

8

"Rusty, dear, we're ready to go cut down the Christmas tree," Agnes called from the doorway to Rusty's room.

Rusty winced. She'd forgotten. "Gran, why don't you go along with them and I'll help decorate the tree this evening."

Agnes eyed her granddaughter.

Rusty sat cross-legged in the middle of her bed, her computer in front of her.

"Trent's coming," Agnes said.

Poor Trent. He hadn't been able to get out of the tree-cutting excursion, either. "Gran . . . Alisa sent me a fax last night, and George—you remember me talking about him?"

Agnes nodded.

"Well, George is up to something with the Next to Nature campaign and I really need to study these pictures." She'd printed them out and they were arranged in a semicircle around her.

Agnes glanced at them. "There's nothing to study. They look like inkblots."

"Sort of, but I can see what George has in mind and it's a good idea. Too good. I need time to counter. Can't I skip—"

"Not after this morning's fiasco in the kitchen."

"Nobody complained."

"They were being polite. Now put on something pretty." Agnes opened Rusty's closet and inspected the slim contents. "This is your chance to make up lost ground."

"But I'd planned to work this morning!"

Agnes tossed a disparaging look at Rusty's computer and plucked an orange sweater from its hanger. "Wear this, it'll give you some color. You're looking peaked."

"I'm looking peaked because I only got two hours of sleep last night!" Giving up, Rusty tugged the sweater on over her shirt.

"I knew I shouldn't have let you bring that computer with you."

"It's a good thing I did!" Exhaling, Rusty turned off her computer and pulled on her boots. "Alisa found out that George is using photography for his Next to Nature presentation. I'm only using sketches. Now I've got to use pictures, too, or my presentation won't look as good."

"So take your camera along today!" Agnes threw up her arms. "Good heavens, Rusty. We're going into the woods to cut down a tree. You don't get much closer to nature than that."

EVERYTHING HE OWNED in the world was at stake on this construction project, yet Trent found himself jouncing along in the back of a horse-drawn cart on the way to cut down a Christmas tree. Clarence and Harvey were driving, he, Doc and the Romero women were sitting on hay bales in the back.

He wasn't certain how he'd been maneuvered into the tree-cutting expedition, but something Harvey had said—and Doc hadn't—and the way Clarence had looked, suggested that they were going to curtail Trent's work time completely if he didn't come along.

Okay, then he'd stay up nights and start sleeping in.

"How about another round of 'Jingle Bells'?" Harvey suggested before launching into the song. "Dashing through . . ." he trailed off. "Snow. You know what we need? Snow for a genuine white Christmas." Harvey abandoned "Jingle Bells" and started singing "White Christmas," his thin tenor augmented by Clarence's growling bass.

Trent and the others joined in. It was difficult to remain unmoved after thirty minutes of Harvey's spirited caroling. Even Doc had smiled a time or two.

Rusty had lost the tight expression she'd worn when Trent had helped her into the cart and was looking around at the scenery as they rolled down one of the many old cow paths crisscrossing this area of the Triple D.

Her lips naturally turned up at the corners, telling him she was basically a happy person. He'd noticed she was easy to be around. Silences with her were never uncomfortable. She didn't sulk, she didn't cling, and she didn't demand his attention all the time.

Feeling vaguely guilty, Trent mentally compared her to the women he dated. They were usually longer, leaner, blonder, and not the type to ride in a hay wagon. Since he didn't plan to use this form of transportation often, that quality wasn't important to him.

The way a woman looked standing next to him was. He liked watching the envious expressions on other men's faces when they saw his latest date. If he'd had to put up with an occasional pout, that was a price he'd willingly paid.

Although she'd never be with him back in Dallas, Trent imagined Rusty standing beside him and was surprised at how easily the picture came to him. She had a city sophistication about her and looks that would be dramatic, rather than merely pretty. She could actually carry on a conversation, too. He imagined her charming his friends.

The thought so unnerved him, he actually shuddered.

"Hot chocolate, Trent?" Agnes Romero offered him a cup from the thermos she'd brought.

"Sure, why not?" The temperature outside wasn't that cold, but it wasn't a summer day, either. "Would you like some?" he asked, holding out the thermos to Rusty.

"Thanks—but don't fill it too full," she cautioned as the cart lurched to one side.

The chocolate was rich and hot. Trent exhaled and let his mind wander—away from women and numbers and bids and legalese. Instead he allowed his body to sway with the movement of the cart.

"How much longer?" Rusty asked, grabbing at the side of the cart when it shifted.

"Hard to tell at this pace. The trip's usually about fifteen minutes by car."

"Where are we going?"

"We're headed to the edge of a piece of grazing land. Years ago, Clarence planted firs there as a windbreak and my uncles have been cutting them for Christmas trees ever since."

"So you've got your own private grove." Smiling as though the idea appealed to her, Rusty sipped her hot chocolate. "I've been looking at all these pines—" she gestured to the towering trees that lined the path "—and I wondered how on earth you thought you were going to get one inside the house."

Trent laughed and started to reply when he noticed three pairs of eyes scrutinizing them. Clarence was still watching the road, but Trent knew he was straining to hear what they said. Great. Every move he and Rusty made today was going to be examined for romance potential. He wondered if she was aware of it.

Instead of keeping the conversation going, Trent leaned back and pretended to drink hot chocolate from his empty cup. He wished he could just forget why Rusty was here and talk with her like a normal person. He had a feeling—okay, more than a feeling—that he could get to like her if the circumstances and timing were different.

"We're here!" Clarence announced sometime later. He drove the horse into a small clearing and stopped beside a wooden trough by an old-fashioned pump.

"It's a little house all alone in the woods." Rusty sounded intrigued.

"An old line shack for hands to sleep in when they were out working cattle," Trent told her as he lowered the back of the cart.

"Does anyone live there?" she asked, turning to him.

"Oh, no. It's too primitive. No more than minimum temporary shelter." Trent jumped down and held out his arms, but Rusty was already in mid-leap.

She landed beside him. "How primitive?"

"Take a look. Uncle Clarence, hang on and I'll be there in a minute." Trent helped Agnes out and offered a hand to Doc, who looked as though he wanted to refuse it.

Agnes, whether deliberately or not, turned away to exclaim over the cluster of firs in varying heights. Since she wasn't watching, Doc accepted Trent's help.

Harvey, clad in his running shoes, bounded out and tended to the horse. Trent saw that Rusty was rubbing at a window and peering inside the old shack, so he approached Clarence.

"I'm getting old, boy." Clarence hefted his weight to the edge of the driver's seat and handed Trent a step stool. After Trent positioned it, Clarence held on to his shoulders and maneuvered himself to the ground, where he stood and wheezed.

"Now don't be telling me I need more exercise," he said when he saw Trent's face. "I get enough of that from Doc and Harvey."

"You should listen to them," Trent replied, more concerned than he let on.

"The only reason I'd need to stay in shape would be if I had grandnieces and nephews to chase after." Clarence arched a gray eyebrow in Rusty's direction.

Trent gritted his teeth. "She can't cook, you know."

As both men watched, Rusty walked to another window and bent to peer inside. A breeze lifted her sweater a few inches above her middle, revealing form-fitting jeans and a trim waist.

"Maybe not," Clarence said. "But who cares?"

"TRENT?" Rusty called. "Is it okay to go inside? I don't think the door's locked." With its weathered gray wood, this place looked like a relic from the Old West.

"It shouldn't be." Trent left his uncle and walked toward her. Clarence grinned and waved at her from behind Trent's back. "However, some uninvited guests from the animal kingdom might be inside."

"I didn't see anything moving," Rusty said as Trent reached the shack and pushed the door handle.

The rough wood screeched before the door gave. No scurrying or rustling sounded, so Rusty followed him cautiously inside. The two outside windows let in just enough light to illuminate the functional interior.

"Not much in here." Trent flipped a light switch. Nothing happened. "There's a generator out back for electricity—"

"This place is wired for electricity?" Rusty asked sharply, an idea beginning to form.

"To a certain extent."

Rusty gazed around the one-room shack. Triple-decker bunk beds with grimy mattresses lined two walls at one end. Never mind. At the other end, a black cook stove straight out of a museum sat beneath simple wooden cabinets secured with hooks and eyes. A water pump curved over a stained porcelain sink. A stone fireplace with all the character one could wish for dominated the rest of the room. What a find.

Trent gazed out the uncurtained window, apparently lost in thought.

Rusty's mind whirled. This shack, though neglected and obviously well-used, was picturesque and she desperately needed picturesque right now. A little cleaning—not much, she wasn't into that—but with some judicious props . . . Rusty opened her camera and with shaking fingers attached the flash. Alisa had to see this.

Agnes had been right. This abandoned shack screamed Next to Nature. Drape some plaids . . . light a fire in the fireplace . . . maybe a bearskin rug . . . and a discreet display of Next to Nature products in the foreground.

Rusty snapped off two pictures.

"What are you doing?"

"Taking pictures." She zoomed in on the black wood-burning stove.

"Why?"

"I like the way the place looks." Rusty lowered her camera. Judging by Trent's suspicious expression, confession time had arrived. The campaign proposal was too important to jeopardize by continuing to play the Happy Homemaker.

At the thought of admitting that she was not here on a husband hunt, Rusty felt both relief and trepidation. She'd need a photo release to use Triple D property in her presentation, but more than that, she'd need time—the time she was spending keeping up the kitchen charade. It was probably pointless now, anyway.

Yet, if she told Trent she had no interest in the lifestyle he sought, what was the point of her remaining at the ranch? He'd be justified in asking both Rusty and her grandmother to leave. She'd lose her chance to photograph his property.

Rusty was well aware of the irony in her situation. She'd arrived wanting to leave as soon as possible. Now she was seeking a way to remain.

Before she could figure out how to state her case, Trent spoke.

"You like rustic and abandoned?"

"I think this place is great," Rusty was able to say in all sincerity. "Antiques like these would go for big bucks in the city. And the view..." She gestured out the windows. Even the grime couldn't detract from the pines and the sloping field beyond. Her grandmother and his uncles looked like storybook characters as they wandered in and out of a small grove of living Christmas trees. "It looks like the backdrop of a painting." Or an ad campaign.

Trent stared hard at her, making Rusty nervous. Perhaps her confession should wait.

He shoved his hands into the back pockets of his jeans, shot another look out the window and appeared to come to a decision. "Have a seat." With a scraping sound, he pulled out one of the ladder-back chairs surrounding a plain, four-legged wooden table.

Uh-oh. Rusty sat.

He took the chair across from her, leaving the table between them as though they were in negotiations. "You come from Chicago, right?"

Rusty nodded.

"Lived all your life in the big city?"

"Yes."

"House or apartment?"

"Apartment. What are you getting at?"

Shifting, Trent rested his forearms on the table and leaned forward. "You know . . . this rugged outdoors environment is new and different to you."

"I'll say."

A corner of his mouth tilted upward. "I always enjoy spending a few days here myself after being surrounded by the concrete and noise of a big city. To you, getting away from it all may seem—" he gestured as he sought for the right words "—romantically appealing, but living here day after day could get boring. It's isolated—"

Rusty held up a hand. "Wait a minute. What makes you think I want to live here? Because I took pictures?"

"Not *here*." Trent drew a breath. "At the Triple D."

"Excuse me, but weren't you looking for someone to live with you at the Triple D?"

Trent sent a glance heavenward. "I can certainly understand how you came to think that." He swallowed. "But, no. And you need to be aware of my feelings before you become too attached to . . ."

"To *you?*" The nerve!

"To the idea of ranch life," Trent finished heavily. "To the 'romantic cabin in the woods' scenario."

Wait a minute. *He* was rejecting *her*. Rusty stared. He was trying to tell her she wasn't the one for him and his domestic fantasies. Well, she knew that. She'd been expecting a talk like this ever since breakfast. How mortifying to realize she couldn't fake domesticity for even a weekend. But she had other appealing qualities, didn't she?

"It's because I can't cook, isn't it?"

Trent gripped his forehead and sighed. "I don't care whether you can cook or not."

"Then it's me." She didn't appeal to him. Rusty absorbed this blow to her femininity with mixed feelings. "Well, you did tell me you weren't interested in me, so I suppose I shouldn't be surprised." *After that kiss, I just didn't believe you.*

"That's not true—" Trent groaned. "Rusty, I'm sorry, but I can't keep pretending any longer. You responded to the *Texas Men* profile in good faith, but the man it described isn't me."

"Who is it? Your evil twin?"

Trent's laugh was subdued. "You're going to get a kick out of this—at least I hope you will—but my uncles placed that ad." He grinned a hopeful let's-laugh-about-it-together grin.

"And you didn't know about it?" Pieces were beginning to fall into place.

"I knew about it," Trent admitted with a rueful grimace. "But I didn't think any woman, any *normal* woman, would respond. But I have to tell you, there are a *lot* of desperate women out there. I couldn't believe it, I mean, that write-up was about as feudal as you can get. Can you imagine any—" He caught himself, his eyes widening.

"Yes?" Rusty arched an eyebrow, enjoying his discomfort.

"I don't mean to imply that *you* were anything other than an unexpected surprise," he said in a game attempt to salvage things.

"I'll bet." If she weren't so relieved to learn Trent wasn't the Neanderthal she'd thought he was, Rusty would be angry. In fact, she might be angry after all.

Trent ran a hand through his brown hair. "I've really screwed this up, haven't I?"

"Maybe not. Let me recap. This was a joke?"

"No! Not a joke. My uncles are completely serious. They've been after me to get married and they haven't liked any of the women I've brought to meet them."

"Have there been a lot of women?" Rusty slid the question in.

"Oh, y—no." Trent shook his head. "Not many. One or two." He cleared his throat and hurriedly went on. "My uncles wanted me to find a real homebody. I told them that women weren't like that anymore and they asked if they could find one, would I meet her, I said yes, never dreaming—anyway, here you are." He stopped, took a breath and said, "I'm sorry, but I'm not ready to settle down at the Triple D or anywhere else and it's not fair to you for me to continue to pretend that I am."

Trent looked her right in the eye as he spoke, she'd give him that.

Rusty let out the breath she'd been holding. "Oh, I am so torn. On one hand, it would be wonderful to have you groveling at my feet, begging forgiveness, but I am a decent human being..." She stopped. Better not push it. "Who needs a favor."

"Anything." He exhaled in patent relief.

"Hey, really?" Things were *definitely* looking up.

Trent narrowed his eyes. "It occurs to me that I've left myself open to blackmail."

Rusty shrugged. "A favor, blackmail, it's all the same."

"I might argue the point with you, but go ahead." His chuckle had a harsh edge.

Rusty toyed with the idea of retaining the upper hand. He'd just told her his profile was a fake, but he didn't know Rusty was a fake, as well. But that would mean she'd have to keep pretending and all this pretending was time-consuming. For both of them. "Will it set your mind at ease if I tell you that Gran answered your uncles, not me? I never had any intention of giving up my career to play house on a ranch."

"You mean . . . ?"

"I'm *not* husband hunting."

Trent blinked twice, then settled back in his chair, a slow smile spreading over his face. "Go on."

"For reasons unknown to me, my grandmother became obsessed with spending Christmas here, and since she couldn't come without me, I said I'd come with her. But I never planned to stick it out for the full two weeks."

"That's cheating."

"Hey, look who's talking."

They grinned at each other.

"So you aren't the homemaker type?" Trent asked.

"What was your first clue?"

"I think it might have been the arm wrestling invitation."

"It's still open."

"I'm still passing." Trent tilted his head to one side. "So, what type are you?"

The desperate corporate type. Perhaps there was a way to mention that she was also a member of the Olympic gold medal kissers fan club. "I'm a not-ready-to-settle-down type."

"My favorite." Trent gave her a frank look that made her insides quiver.

"What a coincidence." A happy, stupendously, wonderful coincidence.

Trent sent a breathtaking smile her way. "You mentioned a favor?"

"Ah, yes." Rusty told him all about the Next to Nature campaign and how she wanted to use the shack as a backdrop for photographs. "So, I would much appreciate it if my grandmother and I could stay a few more days."

"I wasn't going to make you leave," Trent said, surprise in his voice.

"But I assumed that's why you told me the truth about your profile. If we're gone, you can work."

Trent shook his head. "Didn't you see them watching us on the way out here?"

"Sort of."

"It's going to get worse. They expect us to spend time together and I just don't have that time."

"But if we left, you would." Rusty had hoped to acquire professional photography equipment, but it appeared the camera she had with her now was going to have to do the job. There would be no opportunity to get another or to add the props she wanted.

"If you leave, my uncles will just bring in someone else, and I might not be so lucky next time."

"How gallant."

"It's true. The next woman might want to spend all her days cooking and catering to my every whim," he said in a dry voice. "What a horrible thought."

Rusty raised her eyebrow. "Let's not forget bearing your children. Lots and lots of children. You'll spend your nights and weekends lovingly surrounded by diapers, baby bottles and plastic toys in bright primary colors."

"I'm doomed, aren't I?" Trent held his chin in his hand.

"Not necessarily. Maybe we could work together." Real close together. "We could pretend to be spending time with each other, but you could work on your project and I could work on mine."

Trent nodded. "We'd have to get out of the house. I fully expect them to confiscate my computer as it is."

"Have laptop, will travel," Rusty said. "Some place in town, then?"

"Too far away." He thought for a minute, then assessed their surroundings. "How about right here? Once we run the generator, we'd have electricity and privacy. Rudimentary plumbing, but it is indoor."

"Swell." Rusty looked around. "But no telephone."

"I've got a cell phone."

She gaped at him. "You've had a cellular phone all this time? Then why were you putting up with Harvey's interruptions?"

"Because cellular transmissions aren't secure. They can be overheard and I don't want any of my competitors knowing details of my business negotiations."

That made sense to Rusty. "But I need E-mail and fax."

"You can do all that through my cell phone," he informed her offhandedly.

"You can?" There was light at the end of the tunnel.

"My phone has jacks. Reception might be a bit iffy at times, but, yes."

Technology was wonderful. "And you'd let me use your phone? I'll pay you back."

Waving away her offer, Trent stood. "Don't worry about it." He gestured to the window where their relatives were huddled together, sending glances toward the shack. "We can talk more later. Right now, we'd better go look at Christmas trees."

Rusty was euphoric. After this morning's breakfast failure, things had looked pretty grim. Now not only did she have a chance to augment her presentation with dynamite pictures, she'd discovered that she and Trent were on the same wavelength.

Things were going to get very interesting at the Triple D in the next few days.

"I THINK that tree is the one." Agnes had dithered back and forth between two gorgeous firs while Harvey had collected pinecones to grow seedlings and replant. Everyone else was still seated on the ground after lunch.

"Trent." Clarence gestured to the tree. "Start sawing."

Trent popped the last bit of cookie into his mouth, brushed his hands on his jeans, then took a red chain saw out of the cart.

While Rusty cleared away the remains of their picnic lunch, Trent yanked the starter rope on the saw.

With a loud roar the motor leapt to life, the noise making it impossible to talk or even to think.

The whining screech the saw made as it bit into the tree trunk hurt Rusty's teeth, so she wasn't sorry when an ominous clanking sounded moments before blessed quiet reigned once more.

"The chain broke," Trent said, his voice deceptively mild.

"That's impossible," Harvey protested. "The parts are guaranteed for thirty-six months!"

Trent jerked off his safety glasses and set the saw aside. "Make a note not to buy that brand next time."

"But they have a warranty."

"Which I'm sure they'll honor," Clarence said. "In the meantime, see if there's an ax in the shack and we'll cut this tree down the old-fashioned way."

Rusty knew Trent was thinking about how much time chopping the tree with an ax was going to take. She half hoped there wouldn't be an ax, but Harvey had disappeared inside and was now brandishing an old, but probably still useful ax.

"Gran, did you bring anything else to drink?" Rusty called. Agnes and Doc were off trimming branches from the rejected trees for decoration. Had they forgotten about the lighted pine garland Clarence had ordered?

"Look in the cooler," Agnes replied on her way to the cart, her arms full of branches.

Rusty couldn't find any drink cans. "Nothing in here. What about the ice chest in the cart?"

"I'll check." Her grandmother took two steps forward, caught her foot on a tree root and went sprawling.

"Gran!" Rusty raced to her grandmother's side, but Trent reached her first. Doc shoved him aside.

"Agnes?" Dropping to his knees, Doc rolled her over, cradling her against him.

"Stand back, I know CPR!" Harvey yelled.

Huffing and puffing, Clarence ambled toward them. "The woman's still breathing," he affirmed, sounding in need of some resuscitation himself.

"Nothing's hurt but my pride." Agnes tried to sit up and grimaced.

"Gran, you *are* hurt!" Rusty knelt down.

"No—"

"Now, Miss Rusty, you just let Doc have a look," Clarence instructed.

"He's a vet!" Rusty protested as the middle Davis brother ran his hands over her grandmother's limbs.

"It'll be all right," said a voice in her ear. "Doc knows what he's doing." Trent rubbed her shoulders and Rusty relaxed in spite of herself.

"An ankle's an ankle," Doc said. "And this one's sprained."

"Nonsense." Agnes tried to stand, but failed.

"Oh, Gran!" Rusty had never seen her grandmother suffer from anything other than a cold. She looked so frail surrounded by the hefty Davis brothers.

"We're going to take you back to the house now," Doc announced, his tone precluding argument.

Supported by Doc on one side and Trent on the other, Agnes limped to the cart. Doc tucked a blanket around her.

"But the Christmas tree!" Agnes protested, waving at it.

"Don't worry about that, Mrs. Romero." Trent helped his uncle Clarence into the driver's seat. "We can cut it down tomorrow."

"No need for that. I'll just drive them back, then I'll turn around and pick up you two and the tree," Clarence offered.

"I'm going with my grandmother," Rusty said firmly. How could anyone think she'd abandon her grandmother to chop down a Christmas tree?

"Oh, no!" Harvey pulled himself up beside Clarence. "I'm going, so you don't have to. I know CPR," he reassured her again.

"You keep your lips off my grandmother!"

Mouth twitching, Trent took Rusty's arm and pulled her away from the cart. "Calm down."

"I *am* calm!" Rusty searched the clearing for her camera and found it next to the cooler.

"They'll take good care of her." Trent didn't appear unduly alarmed, which set Rusty off again.

"But she's *my* grandmother! I should be with her." She marched toward the cart.

Clarence flicked the reins. "You two just stay here and have fun!" Grinning, he waved.

"Wait!" Rusty ran after them.

"I'll be fine, dear," Agnes called as the cart lurched out of the clearing.

Appalled, Rusty turned to Trent. "Do something!"

He waved.

Rusty watched as the cart rolled away at a brisk pace. "I don't believe this."

Trent retrieved the ax. "I do. Didn't you hear what Clarence said? 'I'll be back for you *two*.' And that was before Harvey got in the cart."

What was he saying? "They couldn't have planned this. My grandmother was really hurt."

"I don't think they planned that part." He toed the cut branches Agnes had been carrying. "But wasn't it fortunate that these cushioned her fall?"

Of all the.... Rusty sighed. She and Trent were alone together—without their computers. It made horrible sense. "So what do we do now?"

Trent hefted the ax. "I guess we're going to chop down a Christmas tree."

9

"HEY, HARVEY, how's it going?" The UPS driver opened the back of his van.

Harvey, barely able to contain his excitement, examined the return address of each box as it was unloaded.

"The deer! Clarence, the deer have arrived!"

Rusty had been in the kitchen with Agnes, whose ankle was much better, bagging Christmas cookies for the parade of delivery men. She knew many by name now and Harvey treated the regulars like members of his extended family.

She walked out onto the porch in time to see the FedEx van pull up. Harvey was delirious with excitement.

Rusty waved to both drivers—honestly, she'd met more eligible men out here in the middle of nowhere than she'd met in the past several months in the city.

"Miss Rusty," Harvey called. "There's a package for you!"

Props for the line shack, she hoped. She'd only sent the film off yesterday and though Alisa hadn't seen the pictures yet, she'd been wild about Rusty's idea to photograph the Next to Nature products there. Still, this time lag was a killer.

Rusty was also worried. According to Alisa, Mr. Dearsing had been asking if she'd been in contact with Rusty, and making some vague reference about moving up the presentations a week.

That was George Kaylee's doing, she knew. He wanted her to be rushed and not fully prepared.

Or maybe he suspected Alisa had discovered his use of photographs and this was his way of retaliating. Whatever, Rusty needed to produce the Next to Nature product pictures immediately.

It had been three days since the tree-cutting excursion. Rusty almost felt guilty that being stranded with Trent had produced exactly the opposite effect her grandmother and his uncles had been hoping for.

Instead of a blossoming romance, the afternoon had resulted in an alliance against meddling relatives.

After Trent had chopped down the Christmas tree, they'd used the time until Clarence returned preparing the shack as an office hideaway.

Now the problem was finding time to use the place. Rusty hadn't been able to get away since Agnes's sprained ankle had kept her off her feet, so Rusty, horror of horrors, had been cooking. Actually, what she'd done was make a huge dent in Harvey's stores of frozen prepared food, but nobody complained.

Agnes and the uncles had done a superb job of keeping Rusty and Trent occupied with garland hanging, light stringing and tree decorating. But today, after lunch, she and Trent planned to go horseback riding. Alone.

Rusty didn't let the fact that she wasn't a horse-woman dissuade her. She needed to take more pictures and work on that ad copy.

As she signed for her package, Trent and Clarence emerged from the house and joined Harvey and his deer.

Picking up two of the white-lighted wire forms, Trent approached her. "Can you be ready to leave at one o'clock today?" he asked under his breath.

"More than ready. Did you get the generator working?"

"Yes." He gazed at her. "Smile, or they'll think we're quarreling."

Smiling through gritted teeth, Rusty wiggled her fingers at Trent's watching uncles.

"I WILL NEVER WALK again." Rusty slid off her horse and into Trent's arms. If she weren't so sore, she would have made more of the situation. But not much more. "I have no idea how I'll ride back to the ranch house, either."

"You can do it," Trent said in a buck-up-old-girl voice. "Remember, we don't have as much time here as I'd like. The trip out took longer than I thought it would."

"I told you I didn't ride," Rusty complained. "Did you think I was going to gallop?"

"I'd hoped for an occasional canter." Trent tied the horses.

"Now I know why cowboys are bowlegged." Rusty limped toward the shack. "Will you please untie the picnic basket?"

"Sure."

There was no food in the basket, just Rusty's computer and supplies, but she'd been trying to avoid suspicion.

Trent handed the basket to her. "If you'll carry this inside, I'll fire up the generator."

Nodding, Rusty took the basket and shouldered her way into the shack.

The generator motor pounded into life, shattering the silence. Rusty sighed. Not the best working conditions, but better than nothing. She should be grateful.

"The place looks surprisingly decent," she complimented Trent when he came inside. She had to raise her voice to be heard over the motor.

"Thanks." His gaze met hers, dipped to her mouth, then slid on past.

For her part, Rusty looked away from his chest, about which she'd had nightly fantasies. "I guess I'll get to work, then."

"Work." He nodded tightly.

They sat at opposite ends of the wooden table, the generator chugging in the background. Rusty wouldn't be surprised if they could hear it back at the ranch house.

She glanced up at Trent to comment about it and caught him looking at her.

A heartbeat later he turned his attention to his laptop screen with such renewed determination, Rusty didn't say anything at all.

He was thinking about her.

She was thinking about him.

She tried not to think about him. Often. Now that they'd established the new ground rules, she shouldn't be thinking about him at all. He had his goals and she had hers. Neither needed a romance muddying the waters.

Unfortunately, Rusty found it difficult to ignore the handsome, ambitious, single *decent* man who sat at the other end of the rickety table.

Decent. Honorable. Solid traits without flash. Traits missing in many of the men she'd met.

She shifted on the hard wooden chair. The fact that all Trent's decentness came packaged so nicely kept him in her thoughts. Instead of the words on her screen, she saw a shirtless Trent answering his bedroom door. She saw his mouth angling toward hers. She felt . . .

Rusty slammed the computer closed.

"What's wrong?"

As if she'd really tell him. "I can't concentrate." Rusty gestured feebly toward the sound of the generator.

He blinked at her, then rose from the table. "Let me check my briefcase. I might have an extra set of earplugs."

"In your briefcase?"

The locks snapped as Trent flipped them open. "Sometimes the noise on construction sites exceeds the government safety maximums."

Rusty smiled at his words.

He withdrew a pouch and unzipped it. "Great for airplane flights, too." Trent leaned over and dropped two yellow cylinders into her palm.

The tips of his fingers brushed her skin and Rusty felt the touch zing all the way to her elbow. Her hand jerked and one of the earplugs bounced to the floor.

"Careful." Trent stooped to retrieve it and replaced it in her open palm.

"Th-thanks." Rusty was horrified to hear herself stutter.

Trent returned to his computer and Rusty stuffed the plugs into her ears.

Tolerable. Definitely better. She gave a watching Trent a thumbs-up and opened her computer.

Thirty minutes later she'd typed nothing but gibberish. Pure gibberish just so Trent would think she was so unaffected by his presence that she was actually coming up with brilliant new ad slogans incorporating the pictures she'd taken instead of fantasizing about him.

He was so close, yet so far. If she ever wrote that for ad copy she would be shot. Yet, it was true.

Rusty knew her legs were only a foot or two away from Trent's legs. She imagined she could feel the heat from his skin. She wanted to touch him and be touched by him.

Her fingertips tingled. Her lips tingled. Other places really tingled. She was *not* going to get any work done.

She closed her computer.

Trent looked up at the movement.

"I'm going to take some pictures, if that's okay with you?"

"Am I in your way?" he asked.

I wish. "No, I'm going to shoot toward the kitchen and fireplace. Let me know if I bother you."

YOU BOTHER ME.

Trent gave up his work on spreadsheets and watched Rusty drape plaid fabric here and there. She added fake daisies to an old teakettle and stapled fabric at the kitchen windows.

She spent the most time positioning empty boxes and bottles of the product she was advertising. Stepping around the chair seat she was using as a stand, she bent over. Trent caught his breath as her sweater gaped away from her chest and exposed her cleavage.

Adolescent though it was, Trent looked and kept looking. The creamy expanse of her neck and throat continued, unmarred by any tan lines. The image that evoked made him sweat. The tanned blond look he'd previously been drawn to seemed common and over-exposed. Rusty's creamy-peach skin was that color because it wasn't exposed to the sun—and other men's eyes.

His mouth was dry. He'd been breathing—rapidly—through parted lips.

Rusty straightened, then grabbed her camera and started photographing the products from every angle, contorting herself into interesting poses that did nothing for Trent's equilibrium.

She was incredibly flexible and he gave up all pretense of working at the computer and stared at her.

She didn't look his way once, but rearranged the products and went through all the angles again.

Trent's favorite pose was the one where Rusty was on her knees leaning backward as though she was doing the limbo.

Or maybe it was the one where she bent forward and arched her back to shoot from below the products.

Occasionally, she'd rake her hair back from her face or shimmy her shoulders to relax them.

Weak with longing, Trent slid down in his seat.

This was torture. Working together wasn't... working. He couldn't stand it. Abruptly slamming his computer screen down, he jerked a thumb toward the door. "I'm going to check on the horses."

Rusty, looking flushed and tousled, nodded.

Trent waited until she'd brought the camera up to her eye before standing and carefully walking out of the shack.

WITH A SLOW, feminine smile, Rusty sat back on her heels. That had gone surprisingly well.

Especially since there'd only been six exposures left on the roll of film.

"*BEFORE* CHRISTMAS? George got Dearsing to agree that the proposals should be presented *before* Christmas?"

"Yes."

"He can't *do* that!"

"Well, he did." From long experience, Alisa knew the routine—deliver the bad news, then wait for Rusty to yell about it.

This time was no different and Rusty appreciated Alisa's perception.

"I'm on *vacation* and he knows it!" Rusty sat on a fallen log. She and Trent were back at the shack, but Rusty had gone outside to put some distance between her and that infernal generator. The stupid thing chugged incessantly and interfered with both phone and fax transmissions.

And besides, being in a state of suspended lust made her cranky. Agnes and the uncles had thrown her together with Trent in an orgy of Christmas preparations. As much as Rusty wanted to work, being alone with him was too distracting, so she usually took the phone outside and walked around.

"Can't Dearsing see that this is one of George's sneaky tactics?" Rusty leapt from the log and tromped back and forth over the dry leaves and pine needles. They crunched with a satisfying crackle. "Doesn't the man know I'm on vacation?" she repeated.

"Uh, George did bring that to his attention," Alisa said.

"Don't tell me...something like, 'I can't imagine why Rusty chose to take these crucial days off,' intimating that I was letting Dearsing down?"

Silence.

"Well?"

"You told me not to tell you."

Rusty lowered the phone and let out a howl of frustration that echoed through the forest. It felt good.

"Rusty?"

She brought the phone back to her ear. "What?" she snapped.

"The pictures turned out great. Who's the guy with the ax?"

She smiled, remembering the tree cutting excursion. "Trent."

Alisa inhaled. "No *wonder* you haven't come back."

Rusty whimpered.

"*SKIING?* Can you believe it?" Trent pounded the steering wheel as he and Rusty drove away from the shack. "I tell the man he's got the bid and he tells me he's going skiing over Christmas and won't be back until after the first of the year. I told him I wouldn't have the paperwork ready until the last week of the year and all he says is sorry, he's leaving. Sorry!"

Rusty had been quiet. She'd ranted at Alisa and had felt better, so she figured Trent would feel better after ranting a little, too. Besides, she didn't feel like talking.

Eventually, Trent was reduced to muttering, pounding the steering wheel and shaking his head.

"Trent."

He exhaled. "Rusty, look, I know I've been running on—"

"Hey, *believe* me, I understand. Dearsing has set the Next to Nature presentation for the morning of the twenty-fourth."

Trent shot a startled look at her. "That's—"

"Christmas Eve," Rusty finished. "He thinks he'll see the presentations in the morning, have the office Christmas luncheon, and then send everybody home a little early."

Silence filled the four-wheel-drive vehicle all the way to the ranch house. The tires crunched on the gravel drive as Trent drove around to the back and parked.

Rusty didn't know how long they sat there before Trent's quiet question broke the silence.

"What are you going to do?"

Rusty shook her head. "I don't know. How about you?"

Trent flexed his fingers on the steering wheel. "I'm going to run some numbers and see where I stand. Which reminds me, tomorrow's Sunday."

"Church and the snow party." Rusty sighed. "I had no idea there were machines that made snow." Or why anyone would want to make it. Rusty hadn't missed the white stuff at all.

"If a product's made, Harvey finds it. But actually, my uncles have been throwing snow parties on the front lawn of the church for several years. It's always the Sunday afternoon before Christmas. The kids love it. There's hot chocolate and funnel cake and the choir sings Christmas carols. Clarence judges the snowman building contest."

"And snowball fights?"

"Of course." Trent smiled. "We hardly ever get much snow in these parts."

Rusty was amused as Trent's tone took on a rural flavoring.

"I was thinking," he continued, "one of us could go to church and the other could put in an appearance at the snow party in the afternoon. That way, we could each have some time alone to work."

Rusty nodded in agreement. She needed to think without having the distraction of Trent sitting across the table. "Sounds like you enjoy the snow party."

"I do," he confirmed lightly.

Rusty imagined him out in the thick of the snowball fights and grinned. "Okay, though I still think snow is highly overrated."

Trent nodded to the kitchen door where Agnes was silhouetted. "This is the third time she's come to the door." He turned back to her. "A good-night kiss might give them something to talk about." His voice was casually nonchalant.

Though her heart threatened to pound through her chest, Rusty tried to match that nonchalance. "Oh, definitely. Definitely," she agreed. "They'll be so pleased, they won't even notice that we're not spending any time together tomorrow."

"It'll be insurance," he said, moving closer.

"A realistic touch," she said, leaning toward him.

Rusty had no idea how realistic Trent intended his kiss to be but seconds after their lips fused together, he abruptly wrenched himself away from her and drew a deep breath.

"That's enough realism for now."

Still recovering, Rusty could only nod.

"WHAT ARE YOU DOING here?"

Trent stood in the doorway of the shack. He couldn't believe it when he'd driven up to find Rusty's blue rental car parked in the clearing.

"Printing out the millionth draft of my presentation." She was standing by his laser printer, which she'd balanced on a chair so the cord would reach the power source. "What are *you* doing here? I thought you were going to church so you could skip the snow party."

"I thought *you* were going to church. You said you didn't like snow."

"Well, I don't particularly."

"Great." Trent slammed the door and stalked over to the table. "What was your excuse for missing church?" He shrugged off his suit jacket.

"Headache. And yours?"

Trent draped his jacket over the back of the chair. "I ran late and was supposedly following them. I'd planned to plead car trouble."

Her gaze swept over him. "That would explain the suit. You can still have car trouble. Smear a little grease on that shirt and everything will be fine."

"I hope so." Trent ripped off his tie and unbuttoned his collar and cuffs.

Rusty was looking at him. Really looking at him. Looking at his body with the type of raw hunger he had never seen on a woman's face. And he felt the same unfamiliar hunger of desire long denied.

Unfortunately, Trent planned to continue to deny that desire. Though he was known for his Teflon-coated heart, after the brief kiss last night, he knew Rusty Romero wasn't a woman he could easily walk away from. Since that was precisely what he was going to do in not so very many days, it was best for him to avoid touching her. Or her touching him.

Or being alone with her the way he was now.

The laser printer had finished, but Rusty hadn't noticed.

Trent's fingers fumbled. He wished she wouldn't look at him that way.

RUSTY HAD A THING for men in expensive suits and laundry-crisp shirts.

Trent rolled up his shirtsleeves as he stared at his computer, clearly oblivious to the fact that Rusty had lost all power of speech and was probably drooling, as well.

He'd looked good in plaid, great in the flesh, but commanding in a suit.

Could she help it if deep down she wanted a man to be stronger and more powerful than she was? She wasn't proud of her secret, but that's the way it was.

Long ago, she'd even had a crush on George Kaylee, which had lasted until the first time one of her ideas was chosen over his. Then he was no longer powerful to her and his attraction for her ended.

But Trent . . . She'd grown to like Trent even without seeing him in a suit and now that she had—

"Are you finished printing?"

Rusty blinked at the printer. "Uh, yes."

He looked at her expectantly, so she disconnected her computer.

"I—I brought some canned drinks," she said, backing toward the door. "I'll just get them out of the car."

Without glancing up from the screen, he nodded, and Rusty fled, chanting to herself.

Calm down. Visualize. Take deep breaths and focus on the Next to Nature campaign.

Rusty opened the car door and brought out the six-pack of sodas. Although cloudy and cool, the weather wasn't unpleasant. She could proof her work outside—away from Trent. Yes, that's what she'd do. Out of sight really could be out of mind.

"MISS RUSTY, you took the new-and-improved, caffeine-free Anderson pain powders for your headache, didn't you?"

"Yes, thank you, Harvey."

Harvey peered at her closely. "You still look pale. Maybe you shouldn't come with us this afternoon."

"And miss the snow festival?" Clarence boomed. "Nonsense. She just needs some fresh air and distraction."

Rusty put her hand to her temple where a true headache throbbed. In spite of her best efforts, she hadn't accomplished nearly what had to be done this morning. A Christmas Eve presentation. That was low, even for George. And Rusty still hadn't decided if she was going to fly back to Chicago, or let Alisa handle the presentation.

Agnes and Doc were whispering together and sending glances her way. Her grandmother approached and took her arm, leading her away from the others.

"Rachel Marie, I've never known you to succumb to a headache."

"Gran, I'm under a lot of stress—"

"I haven't said much about you spending all your time at your computer—"

"I *haven't* spent all my time at the computer! I practically live in the kitchen!"

"So you should be spending every spare moment with Trent." Her grandmother leaned forward. "I saw that little peck he gave you last night." She clucked her tongue. "Pitiful."

If her grandmother only knew. "Gran, we're here because *you* wanted to come here. Have you forgotten?"

"I have forgotten nothing, but I see a young woman throwing away her chance of a lifetime."

Rusty stared at her grandmother. "You've got that right."

"Don't sass me, Rachel Marie." Agnes obviously knew Rusty had been referring to her work. "Whenever we've planned any activities for you two, it's not long before one or the other of you disappears. And now you claim that you can't come to the snow festival."

"Gran . . ." Rusty winced. Harvey's pain powder hadn't kicked in yet.

Agnes's face softened and she felt Rusty's forehead with the back of her hand. "All right, Rusty. Stay here and rest. Perhaps tonight you can carol with us."

Rusty nodded and looked across the drive to see how Trent had fared.

Surrounded by his uncles, Trent tinkered under the hood of his car, embellishing on his car-trouble story. "I'll stay here and keep Rusty company," he offered, wiping his hands on a rag.

This mollified their relatives and they soon departed.

Rusty and Trent watched them go.

"Good work," he said.

"Except that I really *do* have a headache."

"Oh, hey." He looked down at her in concern. "Do you want to stay here, then?"

Rusty thought for a minute. "I left my laptop at the line shack, so I'll have to come with you. Maybe I'll feel better by then."

But she didn't feel better, especially after Trent started the generator. Rusty hated the generator. She hated George Kaylee. She hated snow. She hated the thought of spending one more minute on a campaign she'd had to redo.

She hated feeling guilty.

Still, Rusty took her place at the table and opened her computer.

Trent signaled her and she removed her ear plugs. "I've got to use the phone," he said.

The generator never seemed to bother him. He just shouted over it. Her head pounded at the thought of trying to think with the additional noise. Rusty closed the computer. "You know what? I'm going to stretch out on the couch and see if I can take a nap. Wake me when you're off the phone."

Nodding, Trent had already begun punching numbers.

Carefully spreading Alisa's plaid blankets over the ancient fabric covering, Rusty put in her ear plugs and closed her eyes, never expecting to fall asleep.

A high-pitched grinding roar woke her. Disoriented, Rusty thought at first that her earplugs had fallen out. She sat up and dug at her ears to find Trent at the table doing the same thing.

"What is that?" she shouted. Thuds sounded against the cabin door. A second later, the generator chugged to a halt.

Shaking his head, Trent stepped to the window. "Hey! What are you doing?"

Rusty scrambled off the couch as Trent ran to the door and jerked it open.

A wall of white greeted them. Snow?

"Rusty, climb out the window. Now!" Trent shut the door, straining to latch it again.

Too startled to argue, Rusty ran around the table to the window. The front of the uncles' red pickup pointed away from the clearing. What was going on?

She lost a few seconds while she figured out that the window pushed out instead of lifting up. Unfortunately, years of weathering and disuse had lodged it firmly in place. She pushed, then jumped back when a wad of white spattered against the grimy glass.

Trent ran past her to the kitchen. "Come try this one!" He climbed onto the counter as the light in the room grew dim.

Rusty saw two figures standing in the back of the pickup truck aim the spout of a strange machine. "That's your uncle Clarence and Doc!" Rusty shouted as white obscured the view. Just before the window was completely covered, Rusty caught a glimpse of her grandmother and a gleeful Harvey standing by.

"I know. Get over here!" Trent strained to open the kitchen window, the only one left. "Got it!" The window squeaked outward just as white sprayed it. Too late.

"The bathroom?"

Trent shook his head. "The window's too small and high. Very funny, Uncle Clarence," he shouted through the partially open window. "Now let us out!"

Only the roar of the snow machine answered him.

"Trent!" Rusty had to shout to make herself heard. "It's getting dark in here. Do you have a flashlight? Matches? Candles?"

Trent yanked open cabinets and drawers as the light slowly but thoroughly faded. Giving up, he stalked over to the door and pounded on it. "Let us out!"

Rusty could hear the machine as it moved around to the back and eventually blotted out the thin strip of light that glowed from the bathroom.

And then there was a sudden and eerie quiet. Except for Trent pounding on the door.

"Are you crazy? Let us out!"

" . . . time together." Rusty made out a muffled response.

"Okay," Trent called, his voice taking a tone obviously meant to be conciliatory. "You made your point. We should have come this afternoon."

"If you don't let us out we can't go caroling tonight," Rusty shouted.

In response, there was the faint sound of a pickup truck driving out of the clearing.

Rusty heard a violent bump and an inhaled curse.

"Trent?"

"Over here."

Where was here? "I can't see anything. It's totally black. You okay?"

"Yes." There was a wealth of suppressed anger and frustration in the word. "How about you?"

"I don't know, am I okay?"

She heard a heartfelt sigh. "I hope so, because it appears that my uncles and your grandmother have snowed us in."

10

"MAYBE THEY DIDN'T KNOW we were in here."

"My car's right out front. They knew."

"Then, why?" Rusty's question hung in the black silence.

"For starters, I'd guess they're ticked at us." Trent's disembodied voice was no closer and Rusty assumed he was still by the door.

She wasn't exactly sure where she was. "Good grief, Trent, why didn't you tell me that frolicking in fake snow was so important to them?"

She heard muttering. "I think it's the fact that we lied so we could sneak off to work."

"Excuse me, but I really had a headache."

"You didn't this morning."

The point wasn't worth arguing. It was apparent that Rusty's grandmother and Trent's uncles had figured out that what they'd fondly hoped was a budding romance was just Rusty and Trent carrying on business as usual. And their relatives were angry. "How could they have found us?"

"I don't know. Does it matter?" Resignation sounded in his voice.

She supposed not. "How long are they going to leave us here?"

"Until they feel we've spent enough quality time together, I suppose. Why do you keep asking me these questions?"

"Because they're *your* uncles. For all I know, trapping women for you is standard operating procedure for them."

"Not until they met *your* grandmother."

Rusty squeaked in outrage. "You can't blame this on her!"

"Why not?" Rusty heard something soft smack against something not so soft, followed by a loud and clear curse.

Served him right.

"It's okay. I'll live," he said, his voice subdued.

"What a pity."

After that, the conversation lagged as each dealt with the ramifications of the situation.

Rusty was inclined to blame the influence of Trent's uncles on her grandmother, but then Agnes had been exhibiting latent streaks of romance lately. Snowbound with a handsome man in a remote cabin sounded romantic—especially if they'd been serving something stronger than milk in the hot chocolate at the snow party.

Rusty heard shuffling. "Where are you going?"

"Forward. I'm aiming for the couch where you spent the afternoon snoring," he grumbled.

"I did not snore."

"How do you know?"

"No, the question is, how would you know? The generator was going and you had earplugs in," she noted with smug satisfaction.

"And I could still hear you snore," he maintained.

Rusty smothered a laugh. "That was the snow machine, which brings up an interesting question. I was asleep. How did four people sneak a pickup truck and a snow machine past you?"

Silence answered her. Though he tried to hide it, she knew Trent was blazingly angry at his uncles and frustrated at being trapped. She also knew that quarreling was one way to avoid thinking about the fact that they were alone together.

"My eyes were bothering me and I may have dozed off myself," Trent finally admitted. "I was waiting for a call—"

"The cell phone!" The same thought occurred to both of them.

"Where did you leave it?" Rusty asked.

"On the table."

"I think I'm closer." Rusty reached out in a wide circle and encountered nothing. She took a step, then another. She smelled the musty couch before she touched it. "Here's the couch." Feeling her way along the cushions, she reached the edge. "I'm in the clear. There's nothing between me and the table."

Confidently stepping forward, arms outstretched, Rusty felt a tug against her knees a split second before she remembered that the cord of the laser printer stretched directly across her path.

Her momentum propelled her forward and she tripped over the cord, hearing the sickening crack of expensive plastic breaking as the printer fell off the chair and hit the floor.

"Rusty!"

She heard Trent's cry as she fell into the darkness, arms flailing wildly. She caught the corner of the table, tilting it as she broke her fall.

Trent knocked into the table. Something slid. "Grab the computers!"

Rusty groped toward the slithering sound but missed.

The two laptop computers, followed by a smaller object, joined the laser printer on the floor. "I think I found your phone," she said, trying not to think of the demise of her computer.

"Are you okay?" Trent asked in the quiet.

Physically, yes, but when was the last time she backed up the hard drive on her laptop? "Just bruised." Was all her brilliant new ad copy lost?

"This is no longer funny," he said.

"Was it ever?"

"I suppose there will come a time when we'll look back on this and laugh."

"Yes, after we lure your uncles and my grandmother in here and give them a taste of their own medicine."

Trent made a sound that sounded like a cross between a chuckle and a groan. "They probably thought we'd light a fire or that we had flashlights. I don't think they realized how dark it would be."

"I don't think they thought at all." Rusty didn't feel like being charitable. She searched the floor around her and found the overturned chair and the laser printer. Something slick coated her fingers. "Trent, I think your printer is bleeding."

He actually laughed and she felt better. "Stay still. I'm going to try to find the phone," he said.

She reached out in a circle. "It's not near me."

"Okay, I'll go the other way."

Rusty heard him cautiously sliding around the table. "I suppose the laptops are history."

"You've got that right."

"This is not good." The loss of her laptop at this critical time was a disaster of such magnitude that Rusty couldn't fully absorb it.

"Don't think about that now."

Good idea, but then what were they supposed to think about?

Plastic crunched. "Found a laptop." Trent's knees cracked as he bent down. "The phone couldn't have fallen far...got it."

Rusty heard the breath hiss between his teeth and then several small objects hit various electronic carcasses before rolling across the floor.

"What was that?"

There was a silence before Trent answered. "The phone cracked open. I didn't step on a laptop, I stepped on the battery pack. Those were the batteries."

And the batteries had just scattered to the four corners of the room.

"I don't suppose finding the batteries would do any good?"

"No."

"So we're stuck here?"

"Until the snow melts or they come back and dig us out."

Rusty stopped herself from asking when that would be. "I do not believe this is happening."

"It's already happened." Trent's voice changed direction and Rusty guessed that he'd stood. "Let's push the debris to the edges of the room so we won't keep tripping over it."

"Good idea."

Together they pushed thousands of dollars worth of ruined electronic equipment against the wall, along with the chairs and table.

"Something slickish is all over my hands," she said.

"Slickish?"

"You know, smooth but not wet."

"No, I didn't know, but it sounds promising." His voice was tinged with the barest thread of humor.

"I can't believe you're making jokes."

"What else is there to do?"

Rusty tried for a flip comeback, but the truth was, she had spent the week avoiding being alone with Trent. And now, here they were. Together. No elderly relatives chaperoning. No computers. No light. No distractions. No work they could do. Just plenty of time alone with the man who currently had the starring role in her nightly fantasies.

Not only didn't she feel flip, she could think of quite a lot to do.

HE SHOULD KEEP moving around. Then he could bang into more furniture. Maybe the resulting bruises would distract him from the constant ache Rusty's presence generated.

Quite simply, he wanted to touch her and hold her and explore the body he dreamed about. And just as simply, he knew he couldn't and then just walk away after Christmas. But how could he endure the next few hours with her and not acknowledge the attraction between them?

Blast his uncles and their stupid plan. In the most unorthodox way, they'd found a woman who was dangerously close to being his ideal. And Trent hadn't even known what his ideal was. He smiled in the darkness. Rusty wasn't his uncles' ideal, but they obviously didn't care at this point.

His smile faded. Fighting fate wasn't an option any longer. He was doomed.

He heard her move. "Where are you headed?"

"The couch."

The couch. He gritted his teeth, then came to a decision. "Mind if I join you?" His voice sounded almost normal.

"If you can find me." The couch's ancient cushions puffed.

"Oh, I'll find you." Cautiously, he moved until he felt the cushion at the back of his legs. How far away was she?

He sent his hand on an exploratory foray and found hers on a similar journey. They both pulled back and laughed awkwardly.

"Are you cold?" The temperature was pleasant, with the snow acting as insulation, but one could hope.

"A little," she answered.

"Scoot closer and I'll put my arm around you." His stage directions sounded stilted when he was trying for matter-of-fact, but Rusty moved closer nonetheless.

Trent lifted his arm and aimed up and around in the dark, bouncing against the back of the couch and settling heavily with his hand curving around Rusty's soft shoulder. Her soft, boneless shoulder.

They both sat very still. Trent, for one, was grateful for the dark, because, as his body was screaming to him, his hand was not curving around her shoulder after all, it was curving around her breast. Her creamy-skinned, full, lacily upholstered breast.

What were the chances? What were the odds?

Should he pretend he didn't notice? Casually move his hand? Apologize or not? Wait for her to say something?

It was difficult to think. This was serious and he shouldn't act hastily. Whatever he said now would most assuredly set the tone for the rest of the evening.

"Rusty?"

"Ye-ees?" She'd noticed.

"Uh, sorry." He moved his hand to her shoulder. "My aim was off."

"Oh, I think you hit your target."

He couldn't tell if she was angry or not. "Rusty, it's dark. I can't see."

"You don't need to see. Men's hands have sonar—like bats."

She was mad. Trent reluctantly removed his arm from around her shoulders. "It was an accident."

"Sure it was." She shifted. "The same way I could just reach out like this and *accidentally* grab—"

They both gasped as her hand closed around him.

"Well, what do you know?"

He froze. "Rusty." His fingers dug into the ancient cushions and his mouth went dry. *Don't move and maybe she won't, either.*

Not only didn't she let go, she adjusted her grip.

His heart stopped. His brain stopped. His lungs stopped.

"How long have you been like this?"

"Days," he groaned, then gritted his teeth as her fingers outlined him.

"I'm impressed."

Involuntarily, Trent surged against her and he bit back a moan. "Since I have no secrets left, you should know that you've got about three seconds to move or deal with the consequences."

He heard a soft giggle and her other hand joined the first. "Promises, promises."

Where was her mouth? "Keep talking, Rusty."

"Is that all you want me to keep doing?"

Trent adjusted his descent to the left, touched her shoulder—her real shoulder—then held her head still until his lips found hers.

Usually, he began with a series of light teasing kisses he'd found made women melt and part their lips, eager for more. There was no need to rush the early sensual exploration. Warming the motor made the car run more smoothly.

But Rusty's mouth was open and ready.

And Trent plunged his tongue inside, shocked that she'd aroused him to the point where he'd think of his own gratification before hers.

Rusty didn't seem to mind. Trent tried to pull back to throw in a little light nibbling but she drew on his tongue, keeping the kiss hot and deep.

Fine with him, especially when she matched the movements of his tongue with her hands.

He could kiss this woman all day. All night.

Forever.

He stilled as the word drifted by his lust-soaked brain. He'd known this would happen. Forever. He tested the word again. Yes, he'd meant forever, as in Forever forever.

And ever... ever... ever... His tongue stroked in rhythm with the cadence and Rusty echoed it with her hands.

And then one of those hands found his and moved it to her breast.

"I was getting there," he murmured.

"Yeah, but I figured you were lost in the dark again."

Chuckling softly, he trailed a path down the side of her neck, enjoying the little panting gasps she made, especially since each gasp was accompanied by a spasmodic gripping that nearly drove him over the edge.

They both shuddered when his hand finally covered her other breast.

He felt the lace of her bra beneath the silky fabric of her blouse and the warmth of her beneath it all, sensations he'd never noticed before. He lightly traced the lace through her blouse, imagining the way it looked.

Rusty squirmed and sighed against his mouth.

Trent was on fire.

And they were both still fully clothed in the erotic darkness, where neither could predict when or where the other would touch.

He felt her hands at his throat. "What are you doing?" He heard his voice crack and didn't care. He was surprised he'd been able to speak at all.

"Unbuttoning your shirt. Losing patience with the buttons. Thinking of ripping."

"Rusty." Trent stilled her hands.

"Good idea. You do yours and I'll do mine."

He fought against the mental image of Rusty unbuttoning her blouse. "You can't."

"I don't need to be able to see—"

"Rusty, we're adults. We both know where we're headed. We have to . . . be adult."

He heard a swish—her blouse being removed from her body. He could smell her perfume. He heard a groan. His.

"You don't have to make that speech. I already know it. We're headed in different directions, we have no future, we'll regret this in the morning. Well, guess what? I'd rather regret a night of passion than a night of frustration. Did I cover everything?"

"With one exception."

"What?"

Trent swallowed. "Rusty, I don't have anything with me."

All movement stopped. As the silence lengthened, Trent's hope that Rusty would say, "No problem. Help me find my purse," faded.

What she did say was, "I don't suppose your uncles dropped any condoms down the chimney before they snowed us in?"

"Are you kidding? They *want* babies. Or rather, they want *me* to have babies."

"How do you feel about having babies?" Rusty asked in a small voice.

"I want babies, but . . . not now."

"Me, either."

They sat in the silence and Trent listened to her breathe. "We do have certain alternatives here."

He heard her shake her head. "No. Too high-school-ish."

Trent cleared his throat and inched closer. "I don't mean to brag, but I can assure you that you won't be reminded of high school."

She sighed. "I'll only feel worse than I do now."

"But not until you've felt a lot better."

"I don't think so." It was a whisper.

Rusty was right. They should cool it.

He leaned his head against the back of the couch and imagined her doing the same.

He listened to her breathe in the dark and forced himself to focus on all the reasons why a relationship wouldn't work. The more he thought, the less important those reasons seemed. Maybe they could have a future.

"Rusty, I've been thinking."

"Don't think."

Her words stopped him momentarily. "We feel something for each other."

"Lust."

"It's more than that and you know it."

She was quiet for a moment. Then she said, "It can't be more because I'm not leaving my grandmother. Everyone in her life left her. She's been there for me and I'm going to be there for her. After Christmas, you'll go back to Dallas and I'll go back to Chicago and by the end of the first day at work, we'll each be relieved we didn't do anything stupid." She groaned. "In fact, with my computer gone, I'll have to leave as soon as we get out of here."

Trent was silent. Broken computer or not, he'd known she wouldn't be content to let her assistant handle the presentation, just as he'd known he'd be returning to Dallas to meet with the owner of the construction company prior to Christmas.

She was right.

But he still felt lousy. Resolutely, he pushed aside all carnal thoughts of Rusty. "So, seen any good movies lately?"

RUSTY HAD NO IDEA how long she and Trent talked. Hours, she supposed. Hours spent in the dark learning his hopes and dreams, appreciating his sense of humor, criticizing his hideous taste in movies, and vowing to cancel his vote in all future elections.

Hours when the darkness freed her to confide thoughts she hadn't shared with anyone else.

Hours in which she refused to fall in love with him or think about a future life where they could spend similar evenings talking.

Or making love.

Desire was there in the darkness, thrumming between them like the lowest of musical notes, more felt than heard.

Rusty wanted to touch him. Several times she'd extend her hand until she could feel the heat from his body. But she'd move away before he discovered what she was doing.

After a while, they remembered the bags of munchies and sodas in the kitchen and ate a highly unnutritious dinner, getting crumbs all over. Then Rusty planned a fantasy advertising campaign for Trent's retirement village and he created a financing package for her own advertising agency.

Owning her own agency had been her secret goal, but until she'd talked with Trent, she'd never thought it could be a reality.

Maybe she could use the financing as an excuse to call him after the holidays.

And then what? asked the voice inside her. *You and your grandmother live in Chicago. He lives in Dallas. A relationship between you will never work.*

Which brought her thoughts full circle. She massaged her temple.

"Is your headache back?"

"Sort of. How could you tell?"

"I heard your fingers rub against your hair."

"I don't know what time it is, but Harvey's pain powders have worn off."

"I've got aspirin in my briefcase. Shall I embark on a search mission?"

"Aye, aye, soldier."

Chuckling, Trent left the couch, his footsteps loud in the silence.

Rusty tried to imagine his progress across the shack. "Where are you now?"

"Heading toward the windows. That's where we pushed the table and I'd set the case next to it."

Rusty heard chairs moving.

"Here's the case. That slick stuff got on it, too," he said as he brushed at the leather.

Something occurred to her. "Are aspirin the only pills you have? I want to know what I'm swallowing."

She felt the couch shift with his weight as he sat down and flipped open the case.

"I've got a few antihistamines, but they're in a bubble pack. Here's the toiletry case." He unzipped it. "I've got antacids in a roll, breath mints . . . this is toothpaste, shaving cream . . . moist towelettes."

"Good grief."

"I told you, it's my emergency travel kit. Okay, here's the aspirin bottle. Where's your hand?"

Rusty waved it toward him and banged into his. He placed a small container into her palm.

"Good luck with the childproof cap." He continued digging in his bag.

Rusty was trying to line up the arrows on the cap by touch when she heard Trent inhale sharply.

"What is it?"

Something crackled as he withdrew it from the bag. "I, uh . . . found a condom."

Rusty blinked in the darkness, wishing she could see his expression. He was probably wishing the same thing. "You keep condoms in your *briefcase?*"

"No—I keep a small toiletry bag in my briefcase. The condom—singular—happened to be in the bag." He seemed to feel the distinction was important.

They sat very still, except for a muffled crackle that told Rusty that Trent was turning the package over and over in his fingers.

"This changes things, I suppose." She was thinking aloud.

"It doesn't have to." Trent exhaled. "I think we decided it would be easier if we didn't know what we were missing."

"That's what we decided, all right." At every crackle, Rusty reconsidered that decision.

"I mean, now, I can only imagine how your skin would feel as I ran my hands over your body. That's better than knowing exactly how soft and silky smooth it is."

Rusty swallowed.

"Or knowing how you would taste," he continued, his voice seductively mesmerizing. "Or where you're ticklish."

Rusty knew and those places tingled.

"Or whether you're a screamer or a moaner."

"A screamer? I think not."

"You've got the potential." He gave a mock sigh. "But I'll never know."

"I'm *not* a screamer. There. Now you know." Rusty fanned her face.

"*I* could make you scream." He spoke just above a whisper, wrapping his words around her, using them as a sensual noose.

She gave a shaky laugh. "You're very sure of yourself."

"I'm very sure of you."

She was damp with desire and he hadn't even touched her.

Rusty pressed her knuckles against her mouth. Regrets. This was all about regrets.

She closed her eyes and relived Trent's kisses and his touch. Would she truly rather regret a night of passion than a night of frustration?

Yes.

The instant she made her decision, something warm uncoiled within her, loosening her tense muscles, reducing the pounding in her temples.

"Okay. Make me scream." She tossed the aspirin bottle over her shoulder. "But it only counts if I scream loud enough to start an avalanche."

She heard the briefcase hit the floor. "You're a difficult woman to please."

She inched sideways. "I can give you hints."

"Hints are good." He inched sideways. "Though I'd rather have light."

"But the dark can be full of surprises." Her voice was husky.

"Or hide the location of this wonderful little package during certain crucial moments." His voice was equally husky.

"I'm sure you'll manage to keep track of it," she murmured as his thigh touched hers. She braced herself for his touch, every nerve in her body straining because she didn't know where to expect it.

Trent skimmed his hand along her thigh, over her hip and toward her waist.

Rusty held her breath just as his fingers reached the bare skin above her jeans.

He paused, then explored a few more inches. "You've been sitting there all this time without your blouse and I didn't even know it?"

She giggled. "Surprise."

The discovery seemed to unleash something in Trent. "So you like surprises."

"Don't you?"

Chuckling deep in his throat, he maneuvered her into a reclining position on the couch while he knelt on the floor. Lacing their fingers together, he positioned her arms above her head and whispered, "You have no idea where I'll kiss you next."

Rusty's breathing quickened. She felt a stream of air cool her skin as he blew across her stomach, her neck and her arms. Gooseflesh rose as she tried to anticipate where she'd feel the coolness next.

He kissed her on the side, just beneath her ribs. From there, he set a meandering course of kisses, licks and nibbles that had Rusty straining against his hands.

"Trent, let—"

"No."

"No?"

"Not now."

But she wanted to touch him, wanted to kiss him. Instead she gasped as Trent used his teeth to pull the snap to her jeans apart and edge down the zipper. "Surprise."

Kissing the newly exposed skin, he began a journey upward until he encountered her bra. "Front hook?"

"No," she panted. "Though if I'd known . . ."

"No problem."

Trent continued his unhurried trail of nibbling kisses, distracting her so much that she was barely aware of him catching both her hands in one of his.

"You're goo-ood," she breathed as her bra fell away and he laced their fingers together once more.

"I wish I could see you," he murmured. "I'm imagining creamy white . . ." Catching the lacy fabric in his teeth, he pulled it gently over her chest, then down her ribs.

Rusty heard the tiny sound as her bra slithered to the floor.

Except for breathing—his slow and deep, hers fast and shallow—there was silence.

Every inch of her skin was sensitized and waiting for his touch. She wanted, needed that touch. She began to move, clutching at his fingers and straining to bring the rest of him closer.

"Trent?" she whispered, and heard the pleading in her voice.

"Right here," he breathed next to her collarbone. He kissed her there and along the side of her neck.

Rusty jerked her head, trying to kiss him, too, but he laughed softly and moved out of her reach.

"Trent, *please*." She was begging. Rusty couldn't believe she was actually begging. Usually she was the one in control.

Even tonight, she'd sat in the dark without her blouse waiting for the right moment to taunt him with the knowledge.

But she was playing the game with a grand master.

"*Trent.*" She couldn't stand the suspense.

With a suddenness that caused the air to leave her lungs, Trent drew his tongue from her throat to her waist in one broad stroke.

Rusty quivered.

Trent traced a series of languid circles that inched northward.

Rusty broke out in a sweat.

"I can feel the texture of your skin with my tongue. I can feel your heat."

It was as though his words summoned that very heat. Rusty felt the warmth begin deep within her and spread to her exposed skin. She was on fire and his tongue did nothing to quench the burning.

She stilled, concentrating on forming her words. "If you do not touch my breasts *right this instant,* I will die."

"Or scream?" And Trent's mouth reached her breast—right that instant.

Rusty thought she might die anyway.

She buried her fingers in his hair, realizing for the first time that her hands were free. She clutched at his back and became annoyed that he was still wearing his shirt. "Take this off!"

She pushed herself to a sitting position and fumbled for the buttons, shaking so badly she could barely work them through the buttonholes.

"I'll help." His hands covered hers and she found they were shaking, too.

Rusty pulled his shirt out of his waistband and tackled the bottom buttons, nearly weeping when she couldn't work them fast enough.

Forget it, just forget it. She sought and found the open part and spread her hands over his chest, feeling the hair curl over her fingers. "I've been lusting after your chest for days."

"I know exactly what you mean." There was a ripping sound as Trent obviously gave in to his impatience.

Nothing was slow after that.

They tore off the rest of their clothes, not caring where they landed.

Rusty ran her hands over Trent's body. "I'm trying to imagine how you look."

"I'm concentrating on how you feel," he replied, and proceeded to explore hollows and crevices that made her moan.

At last she sank back onto the couch and he covered her with his body, drugging her with kisses. Soon, even Trent's magical kisses weren't enough.

"I . . . can't . . . wait—"

"Neither can I."

The instant he joined with her, they both gasped and stilled.

Rusty felt profoundly humbled by the sweet rightness of it all.

"Rusty." He breathed her name on a sigh.

"I know," she said.

His kiss held a promise she didn't want to acknowledge. She couldn't acknowledge it. She *refused* to acknowledge it.

And then he began to move, stroking her in the overpowering age-old rhythm of love.

Love.

No.

But just before she lost her mind to the pleasure, her last conscious thought was *yes*.

And then she screamed.

11

A ROARING woke them.

"What's that?" Rusty, entwined in Trent's arms, blinked in the darkness.

"Sounds like a motor. A big motor," Trent replied.

"More snow?"

She felt him shake his head. "They must be digging us out."

"Oh, my gosh! We don't have any clothes on!" She scrambled off the couch.

"Don't panic. We've got a few minutes." Trent sounded calm.

Well, of course. He didn't have to find as many clothes as she did. "Where did you throw my jeans?"

"Hell, I don't know. Not far."

The motor sounded closer. A lot closer. "Trent!" she wailed.

"Here's something." He handed her a wad of cloth.

"That's *your* shirt!"

"Put it on if you can't find anything else."

"Oh, sure. Why don't we just announce to everyone what we've been doing?"

"They won't necessarily assume we've been doing anything." His voice dipped and she guessed he was searching the floor.

She found her blouse draped on the arm of the couch. "Oh, great, we slept on my blouse!"

"Big deal. We've been here all night, they'll expect us to look rumpled."

"Rumpled, not naked!"

"Here, these jeans are yours. Now you won't be naked."

"I haven't found my panties, yet." She had to shout over the noise.

"Maybe you should skip them for now."

Rusty knelt and searched the floor anyway. She found her bra, which was better than nothing. She put it on, along with her jeans. "Trent, are you still naked?"

"No, I found everything."

She heard him step into his jeans. "Even your underwear?"

"Yes."

"Great, you found your underwear, but mine is who knows where?"

"Will you stop going on about your underwear? I've got to get my pants zipped here."

"Need help, big boy?"

She heard a snap. "Very funny."

Gray light began to show around the door.

"All buttoned up?" Trent shouted. "I think we're about to be rescued."

The engine cranked to a stop. "Trent? Rusty? You two all right in there?" Clarence called.

"You mean, other than being mad as hell?" Trent called back.

Shovels scraped against the wood. "We thought the snow would melt real fast." Harvey's voice was full of apology. "We didn't know a cold front would come in."

Great. Everybody was probably out there. Rusty didn't even know if she'd buttoned her blouse correctly and somehow, she knew they'd be able to tell she wasn't wearing underwear. She finger-combed her hair and hoped her makeup hadn't smeared too badly.

Moments later, with Trent pulling and one of his uncles pushing, the door gave and bright sunlight blinded Rusty's eyes.

"Hey, there you go. Come on out, you two." Clarence's joviality grated on Rusty's nerves.

Stumbling toward the doorway, she shivered and shaded her eyes. Doing the same, Trent grabbed her hand and urged her through the doorway. Glistening white was piled high on either side of an escape tunnel. Doc sat in the driver's seat of a yellow digging machine of some kind.

"Now, boy, I know you're mad—" Clarence broke off abruptly.

"Rachel Marie!"

Agnes had used her full name. Not a good sign. "Gran?" Standing in the doorway, surrounded by leftover snow, Rusty blinked against the sun and searched for her grandmother.

At the end of the snow tunnel, Agnes stared at her with a horrified expression, echoed in varying degrees by Trent's uncles.

Puzzled, she turned to look at Trent at the same instant he looked down at her.

Her eyes widened, as did his.

Black ringed his mouth, smudged his face, his neck and disappeared under his shirt. Fingerprints marked where Rusty had fumbled with the buttons. Two were missing. "Laser printer toner," she whispered as Trent turned his back and shielded her.

She stared at her blackened hands and arms and could guess what the rest of her looked like.

The silky slickness that she'd forgotten all about now graphically displayed exactly how Trent and Rusty had stayed warm last night.

"We look like sexual road maps," he murmured. "X marks the spot."

She looked down and felt her face flame when she saw the dark area between his legs where her fingers had explored. An impressively large dark area, she had to admit.

Then she looked at her blouse where two handprints clearly covered her breasts. If she'd kept her blouse on, the prints would have smudged, but no, she'd taken it off and thus preserved the outline of Trent's hands for all to see.

And see they had.

"Let me handle this," Trent whispered.

"I think you already have."

He grinned just as Clarence cleared his throat.

They turned to look at him.

"Rusty, dear." He approached, arms outstretched, a determined smile on his face. "Welcome to the family."

One look at her grandmother's face and Rusty made the only possible response. "Thank you."

THE TONER on her body was a vivid reminder of Trent's lovemaking. Rusty wished she could scrub away the memories as she'd scrubbed away the toner.

Though she and Trent had tried to play down the situation, Agnes and the uncles had been impossible with their pointed comments. They seated a freshly scrubbed Trent and Rusty next to each other at a stunningly uncomfortable breakfast where they were plied with mountains of food while the others sat at the table, drank coffee and watched the two of them. Each time they spoke, even when it was only, "Pass the salt," all conversation ceased and the two were regarded with expectant smiles.

Trent looked as uncomfortable as Rusty felt. In a display of shutting-the-barn-door-after-the-horse-has-left, the two hadn't had a chance to be alone.

And it didn't look like they ever would be.

When Harvey brought out his bridal supply catalogs, Rusty couldn't stand it any longer and escaped to her room. She dragged her suitcase onto the bed and began haphazardly folding clothes.

"What are you doing?" Agnes had followed her.

"Packing. Under the circumstances, I think it would be best if we left immediately."

"Under what circumstances?"

Rusty started pulling clothes off the hangers in the closet. It was time to be blunt. "Trent and I have no intention of marrying."

"But . . . but you . . ."

"What? Slept with him?" She laughed harshly. "We were bored. It's hardly the basis for marriage." Maybe if Agnes believed the words, Rusty could, too.

"Bored? Haven't you ever heard of Scrabble?"

"It was dark!" Rusty slapped a sweater into the suitcase. "Completely dark! There was no way out. You should be glad one of us wasn't hurt stumbling around. Our computers are broken and, obviously, the laser printer. What were you thinking?"

A subdued Agnes sat on the corner of the bed. "I thought it would be romantic. I figured after your computer batteries went out, you two would be forced to talk and get to know one another."

"We talked. We got to know one another." She folded another sweater. "We're not marrying."

"Rusty!" Agnes bit her lip. "I don't believe that you two don't feel something for each other."

"Because it's obvious we felt something last night, right? It was a fling. It's over." Saying the words hurt.

Agnes pushed Rusty's bangs out of her eyes. "You're in love with him, aren't you?"

Her heart pounded. No. Wrong. She was not in love with him. Not. She was simply having a natural hormonal response to . . . laser printer toner.

She ignored the question. "You'd better go pack. There's a flight leaving just after midnight and I booked two seats. I know the middle of the night is inconvenient, but I was lucky to get anything this time of year."

"I'm not going back with you."

"What?" Stunned, Rusty dropped the sweatshirt she was folding.

"I'm not going back before Christmas. There's still so much to do here. And Harvey ordered costumes for us."

"*What* are you talking about?"

"For delivering presents. And the baking isn't nearly done. We promised."

Something had gone wrong with her grandmother. Rusty had simply thought this domestic nonsense was a phase, but it appeared her grandmother was delusional.

"We came here because you wanted me to check out Trent. I checked him out."

"Perhaps too thoroughly."

Okay, that remark meant her grandmother wasn't totally off her rocker. "At any rate, there's no need for us to stay any longer."

"You promised me!"

Rusty folded the sweatshirt and set it in the suitcase. Taking her grandmother's hands, she said, "I said I'd give it a shot, and I did. But my computer is trashed and Dearsing moved the presentations to Christmas Eve. I don't have a choice." She returned to packing.

"We always have a choice, Rusty." Her grandmother stood. "But you're making the wrong one."

"YOU BETTER BE PLANNING to do right by that little gal, Trent."

Clarence sat behind the big desk in the Triple D office. Doc leaned against the window frame and Harvey sat on the sofa, thumbing through catalogs. Trent, as he had when he was a boy, stood in front of the desk to face Clarence.

It had been years since he'd received a dressing down. He'd decided to let them have their say in hopes that it would defuse the situation.

"Has Miss Rusty said what her colors will be, Trent?"

"Colors?"

"For the wedding."

"No," Trent answered shortly.

"But there will be a wedding," Clarence said. It wasn't a question.

"Good breeding stock," was Doc's contribution.

The situation wasn't diffusing. Trent had had enough. "Whether or not there is a wedding is an issue to be decided by Rusty and me. Thank you all for your concern." He turned and strode toward the door.

"Now, boy—"

"Trent!"

Harvey scuttled over to him and thrust a slim catalog into his hands. "This is for while you're deciding," he whispered.

Trent was halfway down the hall before he looked at Harvey's offering.

It was a condom catalog.

IN THE END, Trent drove Rusty to the airport. He was continuing on to Dallas.

"If you change your mind, you can come back anytime!" Harvey had called.

But Rusty wasn't going to change her mind.

"This is the first chance we've had to talk," Trent said as they waved goodbye to four somber-faced people and drove off into the night.

"There isn't much to talk about, is there?" Rusty had been dreading this conversation. Over and over she'd rearranged the pieces of her life, hoping they'd all fit together. But Trent just didn't fit into her life, no matter how much she might wish otherwise.

He slid a sideways glance at her. "I feel we have unfinished business."

"And I feel that a clean break is best." She stared straight ahead.

"Damn it, Rusty, I want to see you again!"

Rusty closed her eyes. For some reason, she found it easier to talk with him when she couldn't see him. "We both know that the only way we can continue to have a relationship is if I give up everything."

"I'm not asking you to give up anything!"

"Oh? So you're saying you plan to resign from your business, forget your retirement project, abandon your uncles and move to Chicago?"

"You're being unnecessarily extreme."

"Maybe for now, but that's what's down the road, isn't it? How else would we be together?"

He was silent long enough for her to know that he'd never considered changing anything at all about his life. "We could work something out."

Men were always saying that "things would work out." And they did because women took care of the details.

Not this time. "I have a responsibility to my grandmother. She sacrificed years of freedom to raise me and I'm not going to abandon her." Rusty ignored the fact that Agnes had elected to remain at the Triple D for Christmas. "And to be able to fulfill that responsibility, I've got to give this presentation my best shot. If I don't get this campaign, then I'll have to try for another one."

"In a few weeks, when things settle down—"

"Nothing will have changed," Rusty broke in harshly. "You'll be here and I'll be there."

"Rusty..."

"This isn't easy for me." Her voice broke. "You—making l-love with you—" A sob escaped. "Darn it! The thought of leaving you is tearing me apart. I can't go through this again and again, Trent, I just can't. It's better that we break it off now. Please."

He stopped at an interchange and looked away from the road to stare at her, his eyes dark with emotion. "Is that what you really want? A clean break?"

"Yes." She made her voice strong. "It's what I want."

ON DECEMBER twenty-fourth at 10:30 a.m., Rusty presented her Next to Nature campaign, illustrated with eight-by-ten glossy photos of a flannel-shirted Trent and the line shack. The clients were impressed by the emotion they heard in her voice and decided that someone who felt so passionately about their product was the person they wanted handling their account.

Rusty went home to celebrate Christmas Eve alone in her undecorated apartment.

On December twenty-fourth at 2:37 p.m., Trent signed a contract with the owner of the construction company just as the man was leaving town for his skiing trip.

Trent went home to celebrate Christmas Eve alone in his undecorated apartment.

SHE HAD TO SHARE the news with somebody. Digging Trent's business card out of her purse, Rusty called his office. When there was no answer, she called his home.

His answering machine picked up and she burst into tears.

She was alone. Alone on Christmas Eve. She'd achieved the vice presidency she'd sought ever since she'd joined the Dearsing Ad Agency. She was going to be in charge of a huge national advertising campaign. She should be happy. She should celebrate. Instead, Rusty headed for the bathroom and took a shower.

WHERE WAS SHE? Trent slammed down the telephone as Rusty's answering machine picked up. Had she landed the account? Was she happy?

Wasn't she interested in whether or not he'd been able to get the contracts ready to be signed?

He'd done it. He'd put together a major deal and hadn't used one penny of Triple D money to do it. Someday his uncles might live at the Ridge Haven Retirement Village. And from now on, the investment community would see that Trent didn't have to depend on Triple D money to swing a deal.

Life was good. He should be happy. Satisfied. He should celebrate.

And he did want to celebrate. With Rusty.

Trent collapsed on his leather and chrome couch. Though new and expensive, it wasn't as comfortable as a certain broken down piece of furniture in a deserted line shack.

He closed his eyes. What had he been thinking? He shouldn't have let her go. He certainly shouldn't have agreed to this "clean break" she wanted.

When two people love each other, they try to work out the logistics. And he loved her. So why hadn't he told her?

No wonder she wanted a clean break. He hadn't given her any reason to want to see him again. He'd been so wrapped up in his project and she'd been so determined to land that ad campaign that they both had lost sight of what was important: how they felt about each other.

With renewed purpose, Trent picked up the telephone.

TOWELING DRY her hair, Rusty walked through her apartment and paused by the answering machine. Someone had called while she was in the shower, but when she listened for the message, she heard only a dial tone. On a whim, she called the Triple D, but the line was busy. Naturally, what had she expected?

She trudged into the kitchen and yanked open the freezer. Great. Christmas Eve dinner was going to be frozen leftover Chinese take-out.

This was horrible. Awful. How could Agnes have done this to her? They *always* spent Christmas together. Here Rusty was sacrificing her happiness for Agnes and Agnes didn't even appreciate it. Rusty was saving her grandmother from spending lonely holidays just like this one.

Except, Rusty was the one who was standing in front of the microwave with a glob of frozen Chinese leftovers on Christmas Eve, while Agnes cavorted on a Texas ranch with three bachelors.

Something wasn't right.

The phone rang. Rusty scrambled to answer it, conscious of the pathetically eager tone in her voice.

"Rusty?"

It was Trent. She should hang up.

"Yes?" She turned out the lights so she could talk to him in the dark.

"I know you wanted a clean break, but I love you. Do you love me?" he asked without preamble.

Silent tears rolled down her cheeks.

"Do you love me?"

"Yes," she whispered, and heard him exhale.

"Then everything else will work out. I promise."

Rusty wanted to believe him. "How?"

"Did you get your account?"

"Yes!" she wailed, then sniffed. "And you?"

"All signed, sealed and delivered."

"Congratulations." There was absolutely no enthusiasm in her voice, but she couldn't fake it just now.

"Okay," Trent said. "We both have jobs to do, so we'll see each other on weekends for a few months."

"But what then?"

"Then...I don't know. But, Rusty, I'm telling you—we *can* work this out."

She was letting herself in for heartache, she just knew it. On the other hand . . . "All right. I don't suppose I could feel any worse than I feel now."

"I feel great! What's the matter with you?"

"It's Christmas Eve and I'm all alone!" she blubbered.

She heard a deep chuckle. "Then I'll fly up there or you can fly down here. It'll work."

"Are you nuts? There isn't going to be a seat available on any airline."

"There will be a way. We will find it. I'm hanging up now. I'm going to call the airlines. You do the same and we'll see what happens."

He sounded so sure. Halfheartedly, Rusty turned on the lights and grabbed the telephone book. The best she could hope for would be to get put on a standby list.

She'd start with the largest airlines first.

"Merry Christmas, this is reservations. How may I help you?"

As Rusty'd expected, she was put on a very lengthy standby list.

"Your name?"

"Rusty Romero." Rusty could hear the woman typing. There was a silence. "Ms. Romero, you're already booked first-class on Flight 476 nonstop to Dallas."

"What?"

"As well as flights 271, which is already boarding, 582, 1156 and 2558. You were also ticketed on Flight 121, but it departed earlier today." There was a pause. "Though the tickets are waiting for you at reservations, if you do not plan to use them, I would ask that you consider others who are currently on our standby list."

"I—I . . . okay." Dazed, Rusty hung up the telephone.

How was this possible?

If you change your mind, you can come back anytime. Harvey. Dear, sweet, dangerous-with-a-credit-card Harvey.

Dancing to the kitchen, Rusty shoved the Chinese food back into the freezer.

"DO YOU THINK they'll be surprised to see us?" Rusty asked as she and Trent snuck into the ranch house at dawn on Christmas morning. It was a white Christmas—but only on the Triple D front yard.

"Who knows with them?" Trent whispered.

They crept inside and hung up fuzzy stockings with glittered names that Rusty had bought at the airport.

Trent plugged in the Christmas tree lights and they put their presents under the tree.

"I suppose I could start breakfast," Rusty said, doubtfully.

"Uh, no." There was no doubt whatsoever in Trent's voice.

"Then—" Rusty bent down and handed Trent her Christmas present to him "—open this."

He looked from the flat package in his hands to her, then retrieved one in an identical size from beneath the tree.

They stared at each other, then tore open their gifts.

"'*Roaming Romeos. Keeping Long-Distance Love Alive,*'" he read.

"It's going to be hard, so I want to be prepared." She looked at him anxiously.

"Finish opening yours," he said softly.

Rusty did and stared at a book by the same author—the book she'd nearly bought for Trent. *The Commuter Marriage: How To Make It Work*. "Marriage? Trent?"

"Marriage."

"Well, if things work—"

"Marriage," he repeated.

"Are you asking?"

"Insisting." He kissed her. "I've known I wanted to marry you ever since I found out you'd been sitting in the dark with your blouse off. I have a feeling life with you will be full of surprises." He grinned. "Noisy, too."

"I'm not altogether sure you should be allowed to get your own way in this," she said, feeling her face heat.

"So what do you plan to do about it?"

"You'll just have to marry me instead."

"If you insist."

They laughed and kissed, which is where Harvey found them when he tiptoed into the den.

"Oh, oh." He clapped when he saw them. "So you're getting married?"

When they nodded, he turned to alert the others, then caught sight of the stockings by the fireplace. "Oh, look! My name!"

Rusty saw him quiver in delight. How a man could be so wise, yet so innocent at the same time was something she marveled at and was grateful for. She shared a smile with Trent just as the others appeared.

"Trent, my boy, I'm glad to see that you're the man I thought you were." Clarence clasped them both on the shoulders.

Trent smiled down at Rusty. "Only because I found the right woman."

"Oh, Rusty, you came back!" Agnes hugged her. "I'm so glad. You see, I have news."

"What news?"

Her grandmother left her and went to stand beside the silent Doc, who put his arm around her. Her cheeks pinkening attractively, Agnes smiled up at the man next to her.

"Gran?"

Agnes Romero held out her hand.

Rusty clutched Trent's arm as she caught sight of a diamond matching the twinkle in Doc's eye.

"Your grandmother and I are getting married," Doc said to a stunned Rusty.

"And that's not a cubic zirconia, either," announced Harvey. "I have the appraisal certificate."

After a round of congratulations, Rusty, still stunned, still unable to believe that her grandmother was actually marrying one of Trent's uncles, asked, "So you're staying here—for good?"

"For better or worse," replied her grandmother with an adoring look at Doc.

"I told you things would work out," Trent murmured next to Rusty's ear.

"Did you know?"

He shook his head just as Clarence cleared his throat. "All right everyone, time to eat breakfast and change into the costumes!" he ordered.

"What costumes?" Trent and Rusty asked in unison.

The others looked at them in surprise. "The Santa costumes for when we deliver the presents," Harvey said. "They're out in the barn."

"The barn is full of presents?"

"Oh, yes. Lots and lots of presents." Harvey retrieved one of his ubiquitous notebooks. "I have the inventory right here. The tractor for the high school and the ultrasound machine for the veterans home are the big ones this year." He stopped and looked at Trent. "But you two saw it all, didn't you?"

"I . . ." Trent looked down at Rusty and she smiled, knowing he was relieved to have an explanation for all the merchandise his uncles had stockpiled.

"Yes," he said. "Yes, we did." Turning back to Harvey, he asked, "Are you renting a truck? How are you getting all that stuff loaded and delivered?"

"Don't be silly, Trent!" Laughing, Harvey waved his hands and followed Doc, Agnes and Clarence out of the room. "That's what the elves are for."

"Elves?" Rusty and Trent looked at each other.

"I wonder where he ordered them from," she said.

"I wonder how much they cost," he said.

"I don't know, but they probably get time-and-a-half for working on Christmas Day."

"Double if they're wearing tights and pointy shoes."

Laughing, they started for the kitchen. "Hey, wait a minute." Trent stopped her and took her into his arms. "I skimmed that commuter marriage book while I was standing in line and one of the tips was to make each moment you have alone count." He looked around and whispered, "We're alone."

Rusty pulled his head to hers. "So start making it count."

INSTANT WIN 4229 SWEEPSTAKES
OFFICIAL RULES

1. NO PURCHASE NECESSARY. YOU ARE DEFINITELY A WINNER. For eligibility, play your instant win ticket and claim your prize as per instructions contained thereon. If your "Instant Win" ticket is missing or you wish another, send a self-addressed, stamped envelope (WA residents need not affix return postage) to: Instant Win 4229 Ticket, P.O. Box 9045, Buffalo, NY 14269-9045 in the U.S., and in Canada, P.O. Box 609, Fort Erie, Ontario, L2A 5X3. Only one (1) "Instant Win" ticket will be sent per outer mailing envelope. Requests received after 12/30/96 will not be honored.

2. Prize claims received after 1/15/97 will be deemed ineligible and will not be fulfilled. The exact prize value of each instant win ticket will be determined by comparing returned tickets with a prize value distribution list that has been preselected at random by computer. Prizes are valued in U.S. currency. For each one million, or part thereof, tickets distributed, the following prizes will be made available: 1 at $2,500 cash; 1 at $1,000 cash; 3 at $250 cash each; 5 at $50 cash each; 10 at $25 cash each; 1,000 at $1 cash each; and the balance at 50¢ cash each. Unclaimed prizes will not be awarded.

3. Winner claims are subject to verification by D. L. Blair, Inc., an independent judging organization whose decisions on all matters relating to this sweepstakes are final. Any returned tickets that are mutilated, tampered with, illegible or contain printing or other errors will be deemed automatically void. No responsibility is assumed for lost, late, nondelivered or misdirected mail. Taxes are the sole responsibility of winners. Limit: One (1) prize to a family, household or organization.

4. Offer open only to residents of the U.S. and Canada, 18 years of age or older, except employees of Harlequin Enterprises Limited, D. L. Blair, Inc., their agents and members of their immediate families. All federal, state, provincial, municipal and local laws apply. Offer void in Puerto Rico, the province of Quebec and wherever prohibited by law. All winners will receive their prize by mail. Taxes and/or duties are the sole responsibility of the winners. No substitution for prizes permitted. Major prize winners may be asked to sign and return an Affidavit of Eligibility within 30 days of notification. Noncompliance within this time or return of affidavit as undeliverable may result in disqualification, and prize may never be awarded. By acceptance of a prize, winners consent to the use of their names, photographs or other likeness for purposes of advertising, trade and promotion on behalf of Harlequin Enterprises Limited, without further compensation, unless prohibited by law. In order to win a prize, residents of Canada will be required to correctly answer a time-limited arithmetical skill-testing question to be administered by mail.

5. For a list of major prize winners (available after 2/14/97), send a self-addressed, stamped envelope to: "Instant Win 4229 Sweepstakes" Major Prize Winners, P.O. Box 4200, Blair, NE 68009-4200, U.S.A.

MILLION DOLLAR SWEEPSTAKES
OFFICIAL RULES
NO PURCHASE NECESSARY TO ENTER

1. To enter, follow the directions published. Method of entry may vary. For eligibility, entries must be received no later than March 31, 1998. No liability is assumed for printing errors, lost, late, non-delivered or misdirected entries.
   To determine winners, the sweepstakes numbers assigned to submitted entries will be compared against a list of randomly, preselected prize winning numbers. In the event all prizes are not claimed via the return of prize winning numbers, random drawings will be held from among all other entries received to award unclaimed prizes.

2. Prize winners will be determined no later than June 30, 1998. Selection of winning numbers and random drawings are under the supervision of D. L. Blair, Inc., an independent judging organization whose decisions are final. Limit: one prize to a family or organization. No substitution will be made for any prize, except as offered. Taxes and duties on all prizes are the sole responsibility of winners. Winners will be notified by mail. Odds of winning are determined by the number of eligible entries distributed and received.

SWP-H12CFR

3. Sweepstakes open to residents of the U.S. (except Puerto Rico), Canada and Europe who are 18 years of age or older, except employees and immediate family members of Torstar Corp., D. L. Blair, Inc., their affiliates, subsidiaries, and all other agencies, entities, and persons connected with the use, marketing or conduct of this sweepstakes. All applicable laws and regulations apply. Sweepstakes offer void wherever prohibited by law. Any litigation within the province of Quebec respecting the conduct and awarding of a prize in this sweepstakes must be submitted to the Régie des alcools, des courses et des jeux. In order to win a prize, residents of Canada will be required to correctly answer a time-limited arithmetical skill-testing question to be administered by mail.

4. Winners of major prizes (Grand through Fourth) will be obligated to sign and return an Affidavit of Eligibility and Release of Liability within 30 days of notification. In the event of non-compliance within this time period or if a prize is returned as undeliverable, D. L. Blair, Inc. may at its sole discretion, award that prize to an alternate winner. By acceptance of their prize, winners consent to use of their names, photographs or other likeness for purposes of advertising, trade and promotion on behalf of Torstar Corp., its affiliates and subsidiaries, without further compensation unless prohibited by law. Torstar Corp. and D. L. Blair, Inc., their affiliates and subsidiaries are not responsible for errors in printing of sweepstakes and prize winning numbers. In the event a duplication of a prize winning number occurs, a random drawing will be held from among all entries received with that prize winning number to award that prize.

5. This sweepstakes is presented by Torstar Corp., its subsidiaries and affiliates in conjunction with book, merchandise and/or product offerings. The number of prizes to be awarded and their value are as follows: Grand Prize — $1,000,000 (payable at $33,333.33 a year for 30 years); First Prize — $50,000; Second Prize — $10,000; Third Prize — $5,000; 3 Fourth Prizes — $1,000 each; 10 Fifth Prizes — $250 each; 1,000 Sixth Prizes — $10 each. Values of all prizes are in U.S. currency. Prizes in each level will be presented in different creative executions, including various currencies, vehicles, merchandise and travel. Any presentation of a prize level in a currency other than U.S. currency represents an approximate equivalent to the U.S. currency prize for that level, at that time. Prize winners will have the opportunity of selecting any prize offered for that level; however, the actual non U.S. currency equivalent prize if offered and selected, shall be awarded at the exchange rate existing at 3:00 P.M. New York time on March 31, 1998. A travel prize option, if offered and selected by winner, must be completed within 12 months of selection and is subject to: traveling companion(s) completing and returning of a Release of Liability prior to travel; and hotel and flight accommodations availability. For a current list of all prize options offered within prize levels, send a self-addressed, stamped envelope (WA residents need not affix postage) to: MILLION DOLLAR SWEEPSTAKES Prize Options, P.O. Box 4456, Blair, NE 68009-4456, USA.

6. For a list of prize winners (available after July 31, 1998) send a separate, stamped, self-addressed envelope to: MILLION DOLLAR SWEEPSTAKES Winners, P.O. Box 4459, Blair, NE 68009-4459, USA.

EXTRA BONUS PRIZE DRAWING
NO PURCHASE OR OBLIGATION NECESSARY TO ENTER

7. The Extra Bonus Prize will be awarded in a random drawing to be conducted no later than 5/30/98 from among all entries received. To qualify, entries must be received by 3/31/98 and comply with published directions. Prize ($50,000) is valued in U.S. currency. Prize will be presented in different creative expressions, including various currencies, vehicles, merchandise and travel. Any presentation in a currency other than U.S. currency represents an approximate equivalent to the U.S. currency value at that time. Prize winner will have the opportunity of selecting any prize offered in any presentation of the Extra Bonus Prize Drawing; however, the actual non U.S. currency equivalent prize, if offered and selected by winner, shall be awarded at the exchange rate existing at 3:00 P.M. New York time on March 31, 1998. For a current list of prize options offered, send a self-addressed, stamped envelope (WA residents need not affix postage) to: Extra Bonus Prize Options, P.O. Box 4462, Blair, NE 68009-4462, USA. All eligibility requirements and restrictions of the MILLION DOLLAR SWEEPSTAKES apply. Odds of winning are dependent upon number of eligible entries received. No substitution for prize except as offered. For the name of winner (available after 7/31/98), send a self-addressed, stamped envelope to: Extra Bonus Prize Winner, P.O. Box 4463, Blair, NE 68009-4463, USA.

SWP-H12CF1

Cowboys and babies

Roping, riding and ranching are part of cowboy life. Diapers, pacifiers and formula are not!

At least, not until three sexy cowboys from three great states face their greatest challenges and rewards when confronted with a little bundle of joy.

#617 THE LAST MAN IN MONTANA (January)
#621 THE ONLY MAN IN WYOMING (February)
#625 THE NEXT MAN IN TEXAS (March)

Fan favorite Kristine Rolofson has created a wonderful miniseries with all the appeal of the great American West and the men and women who love the land.

Three rugged cowboys, three adorable babies—what heroine could resist!

Available wherever Harlequin books are sold.

HARLEQUIN® *Temptation*

Free Gift Offer

With a Free Gift proof-of-purchase
from any Harlequin® book, you can receive
a beautiful cubic zirconia pendant.

This stunning marquise-shaped stone is a genuine cubic
zirconia—accented by an 18" gold tone necklace.
(Approximate retail value $19.95)

Send for yours today...
compliments of ◆HARLEQUIN®

To receive your free gift, a cubic zirconia pendant, send us one original proof-of-purchase, photocopies not accepted, from the back of any Harlequin Romance®, Harlequin Presents®, Harlequin Temptation®, Harlequin Superromance®, Harlequin Intrigue®, Harlequin American Romance®, or Harlequin Historicals® title available in August, September or October at your favorite retail outlet, together with the Free Gift Certificate, plus a check or money order for $1.65 U.S./$2.15 CAN. (do not send cash) to cover postage and handling, payable to Harlequin Free Gift Offer. We will send you the specified gift. Allow 6 to 8 weeks for delivery. Offer good until December 31, 1996, or while quantities last. Offer valid in the U.S. and Canada only.

Free Gift Certificate

Name: _____

Address: _____

City: _____ State/Province: _____ Zip/Postal Code: _____

Mail this certificate, one proof-of-purchase and a check or money order for postage and handling to: HARLEQUIN FREE GIFT OFFER 1996. In the U.S.: 3010 Walden Avenue, P.O. Box 9071, Buffalo NY 14269-9057. In Canada: P.O. Box 604, Fort Erie, Ontario L2Z 5X3.

FREE GIFT OFFER   084-KMFR

ONE PROOF-OF-PURCHASE
To collect your fabulous FREE GIFT, a cubic zirconia pendant, you must include this
original proof-of-purchase for each gift with the properly completed Free Gift Certificate.

084-KMFR

1997
Reader's Engagement Book
A calendar of important dates
and anniversaries for readers to use!

Informative and entertaining—with notable
dates and trivia highlighted throughout the year.

Handy, convenient, pocketbook size to help you
keep track of your own personal important dates.

Added bonus—contains $5.00 worth of coupons
for upcoming Harlequin and Silhouette books.
This calendar more than pays for itself!

Available beginning in November at
your favorite retail outlet.

HARLEQUIN® Silhouette®

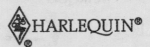